FRITZ

RODNEY WETZEL

ARCHWAY
PUBLISHING

Copyright © 2017 Rodney Wetzel.

All rights reserved. No part of this book may be used
or reproduced by any means, graphic, electronic, or
mechanical, including photocopying, recording, taping or
by any information storage retrieval system without the
written permission of the author except in the case of brief
quotations embodied in critical articles and reviews.

This is a work of fiction. All of the characters, names, incidents,
organizations, and dialogue in this novel are either the
products of the author's imagination or are used fictitiously.
Archway Publishing books may be ordered
through booksellers or by contacting:

Archway Publishing
1663 Liberty Drive
Bloomington, IN 47403
www.archwaypublishing.com
1 (888) 242-5904

Because of the dynamic nature of the Internet, any web
addresses or links contained in this book may have changed
since publication and may no longer be valid. The views
expressed in this work are solely those of the author and do
not necessarily reflect the views of the publisher, and the
publisher hereby disclaims any responsibility for them.

Any people depicted in stock imagery provided
by Thinkstock are models, and such images are
being used for illustrative purposes only.
Certain stock imagery © Thinkstock.

ISBN: 978-1-4808-5311-9 (sc)
ISBN: 978-1-4808-5310-2 (e)

Library of Congress Control Number: 2017915626

Print information available on the last page.

Archway Publishing rev. date: 10/18/2017

Dedicated to my wonderful wife Connie,
who never stopped believing.

PREFACE

The sun hung in the morning sky like some large orange balloon. It sat hidden behind a thick blanket of mist that covered the earth a silent white. Stone lions sat quietly searching out over the worn and tattered head stones of Parksville Cemetery. Their eyes held the sight in a cold glare, noble faces taut with undaunted expressions of strength and dignity. The mist that condensed in the corner of their eyes formed into droplets that seemed to make the pair of sentinels appear to weep.

Somewhere close, the cry of a hawk as it circled for the kill, filled the morning air with sound, but only for a moment. Then the silence, like the mist, lay thick upon the earth again. This silence was known all too well to the mighty felines. If they could speak, they would tell the tale of over a hundred years of such silence. Parksville Cemetery was all but forgotten to the people of the town, lost in the wooded area just two miles from the heart of downtown. It had been unattended for over fifty years. Though many ancestors of today's population lay there in the forgotten ground, no one came to flower or brighten the graves of their past.

If the lions could speak, they would have long ago warned the people of the town, they would have told the secret they alone held. The secret of he who once rested in his unsettled grave, the one they had been put there to watch, the one who had returned. Yet, if they had warned of such things, none would have believed them. Not then, only now, after the horror had begun would they have believed, and of course, now it was far too late.

There is a struggle everlasting between the holy and the profane. Though many a battle is fought, the war still goes on. Now is the time for one more such battle and the lions have called upon their general for hope. Only to their beck-and-call will he answer and indeed the battle be joined.

PARKSVILLE, MICHIGAN

1987

THURSDAY

Philip Parker awoke in a pool of cold sweat. A scream had built up somewhere in the back of his throat and although he was awake, the shriek escaped before the realization set in. It pierced the early morning air and he sat up in his bed. He looked around his familiar bedroom still shaking. Gradually he began to regain some of his composure. The nightmare was already fading, blurring from memory like the sun rising in the mist.

He tried his best to grasp onto it but it just slipped away until nothing remained. Never before had he been so terrified by a dream and now he could not remember what it was about or if it had any bearing on his life. Phillip liked to scrutinize his dreams. Like many people, he thought there was some meaning to what his subconscious was telling him. This dream, or nightmare was not going to be submitted to analysis, however, because it was gone. The only thing that remained now was the fear.

Bzzzzzz.

Philip jumped at the sound of his digital alarm. He reached over and switched it off, then returned to the comfort of his down pillow. His head ached, and for a moment he thought about calling in sick. In the fifteen years he had taught at Parksville University, he had never taken a sick day. "I need a day to myself," he thought. "Maybe a day off would help me get back into focus. Just one long peaceful, restful day." He looked over at the phone that rested next to the alarm clock on the nightstand, started to reach for it, and then thought better of it. Spring vacation would start in just a couple of days. Perhaps he would take a few days off then and visit his sister down in Florida. It would be good to get out of Parksville for a little while. In the back of his mind, Philip already knew this trip was never going to happen, but the thought of it gave him some comfort. Although he treasured his sister, Mary, dearly, her husband, Tom, was another story altogether. He was one of those people who had to be correct about everything and was always eager to give you the advantage of his knowledge. He was precisely the kind of individual that Philip detested the most.

After a good extensive stretch, Philip pulled back the damp sheet and rose out of bed into the cool spring air. He always shut the heat off in his bedroom because he slept well in the cold. Walking briskly to the bathroom, he rapidly turned on the shower, left to the sink, brushed his teeth, took a pee, felt the shower to see if it had warmed and stepped in. The hot water that cascaded down his body was refreshing and, momentarily, Philip began to feel like his old self. It was amusing to Philip how a shower makes a person come alive and ready to face another long hard day. After ten minutes of heavenly bliss, he stepped out of the shower a new man, ready to face all the trials of the day before him. Pausing in front of the full-length mirror on the back of the door, he witnessed his naked body and sighed. Philip could remember when he was able to turn the head of many a fledgling lady, now his body exhibited the signs of aging. His flush belly had become rounded, his arms were just a little flabby and even his penis had seemed to lose its charm. He had really let himself go after Elly's death. How proud and straight his member would get at the slightest touch from her small tender hands. Five years now, and it had yet to come to form.

Elly Parker had been his world, his motivation to live. They had met in college: he a senior and she a junior at a war demonstration in front of the administration building. There she was with her red white and blue striped head band, tight jeans, flip flops, and tie-die tee-shirt. He was in love with her from the very instant he had lain eyes on her. Her tiny frame draped in her long, straight almond colored brown hair. And those eyes, those stunning brown eyes could melt your heart. Within five months, they were married and living in their dream home in the very town where Philip had grown up. Philip went on to get his Ph.D. at good old Parksville University, and for ten years, they were as content as any twosome could possibly be. They had even decided not to have children so that their lives could remain uncluttered and unrestricted: just the two of them.

Now, looking back, Philip knew he did not blame himself any longer for her death. She had adored the Harley as much as he did and their extended rides in the country had been some of their finest moments together. Who could have known that a drunk on a noon-time snoot would be sharing the highway with them that day? Philip could still hear her screams as the bike left the road and headed straight for the tree. The guilt Philip felt now was for cheating. When he admired a woman's breast, it was Elly's breast he saw. When he looked into their eyes, it was Elly's eyes looking back at him. Every time he felt aroused, it was for the wife he had lost in that accident so long ago. To feel anything for anyone else would have been cheating, giving his heart to someone other than the one person he said he would love forever.

"There is no God," he said aloud, "forty-two and impotent."

From the bathroom he made his way to the spare bedroom, which Phillip used as a closet of sorts. It was a quaint little room that Elly had decorated in antiques she had collected through the years. There was an old, turn-of-the-century vanity against the far wall, an old foot-peddled sewing machine that still had a Sears and Roebuck's warranty in one of its drawers, a dresser that she'd bought from an elderly lady down the street, and of course, the canopy bed.

His life had become a mundane existence. Every Saturday he did the laundry. He transported his clothes there to fold, iron, and hang. He would then lay out the entire week's wardrobe by day: pants, shirts, socks, tie, (though he often threw that to the side when the time came), and underwear. He'd place these skillfully on the bed. He owned two pairs of dress shoes, one black and one brown, which he kept at the foot of the bed with his belts, one black and one brown, on top of the bed just above his shoes. His keys and wallet were always on the dresser where he had put them the night before. The mornings took no thought, only motion. Once completely dressed, it was into the car, right on Main, left on Union and then straight on to the college.

Thank goodness it was an early spring this year, he pondered, as he made the left onto Union. Last year they had snow at this time, and everyone was sick of winter. It just seemed to cling on as long as it could to make everyone's life miserable. This year, they had warm days (all the way up to the mid-seventies, the day before) and cool evenings.

Once arrived at the university, it was time to go to the cafeteria in the main building for his coffee. If there was one thing they did fine, it was coffee.

Then it was the long walk down the hall to his office to pick up his transcripts, out the back door, down the walkway to the Ford Historical Building, through the main doors, left down the first hall and a quick right into his class room. He could make this entire morning happen in his slumber. He often thought to himself that if he were ever to go blind, he wouldn't need a dog; he knew it all by heart.

Philip arrived early to class as he did every day. He liked the feeling of anticipation. Looking out over the vacant rows of desks and chairs, he would wonder who would be the first to arrive so he could carry on a swift conversation with them before class. Unlike most of his peers, Philip held a true passion for his students. He thought all teachers started with feelings of caring and interest, but as time went on, they seemed to lose this sentiment through years of repetition. He, however, never had, and it showed to both his students and to his peers.

Despite what he thought, his bushy, straw-colored hair and bright blue eyes still turned the head of many a female student. Often that first student would be a young lady in search of more than academic truth. Such was the case this particular morning.

Sue Barkley had a classic case of a teacher-crush on Professor Parker. She was a senior, and her major was in anthropology. Parker's class on world religions had been required, but Sue knew she would have taken it anyway. Besides being a hunk, Philip Parker was probably the best mind P.U. had to offer. She never let Philip know just how she really felt and usually, like this morning, conversation stuck to academic subject matter.

By eight o'clock, the class was almost full. Philip looked up at the round clock on the wall. He had often wondered if all schools bought their clocks at the same place, for no matter what school you went to, from elementary to college, all those damn clocks looked exactly the same.

"Good morning," said Philip.

"Good morning," responded the class in near harmonic tones.

Philip looked out over the sea of eyes. "Where did I leave off yesterday?" he asked. "Does anyone remember?"

Franky Lake responded with a squeaky, "witches," and curled his hands into claws while pinching his face up into a savage snarl.

The class laughed, and even Philip could not suppress a grin.

"Right, witches," he stated, "and thank you Mr. Lake for your bad dramatization."

The class broke into another brief bit of laughter.

"I do not want to finish this time period without first covering the Inquisition. Franky, what can you tell us about Europe in the fourteenth century?"

Franky pondered the question for a moment. He was considered the class clown. To look at him one might think that the boy was slow, and with his long red stringy hair that was always hanging in his eyes, one might even think him some kind of sixties burnout. However, anyone who had ever had or taught a class with him in it knew that he was as smart as they come.

"Well, that time period was somewhat of an evil age.

"Evil? Evil in what way?"

"Well, around five-hundred thousand people were murdered for heresy or witchcraft."

"I see you have done a little reading ahead Mr. Lake."

"Yes, I have. It was interesting stuff. I was just going to read the beginning of that next chapter and wound up reading the whole thing."

Philip began to speak, but Franky broke in: "Weird, man."

"Yes Mr. Lake, history has many weird periods," Philip finally managed, and Franky nodded.

"Have any of the rest of you read the next chapter?"

There was no response.

"Good. I want you all to spend the rest of the class period writing down everything you think you know about witches and witchcraft. I want you to retell all the stories you've heard when you were kids, I want to know what scared you about these stories. And lastly, I want to know what you believe about the subject. That's it, an easy assignment, so get started."

For the next fifty minutes, Philip sat and watched as students wrote. Sue Barkley kept looking up at the ceiling as if all the answers were written there in invisible ink that only she could see. Christy Carter pulled on her earring trying to switch on her brain. John Hudson was tapping his nose with a pen, trying to beat the answers in, while Tommy Tucker kept his leg in a continuous vibrating motion.

This was what it was all about. Yes, his life was mundane; yes, he was in a rut; yes, he could go through his life with his eyes shut; yes, he had no social life; and yes, he was probably impotent. But this, this moment, forcing young people to use their minds to see the process, to know that because of him, they are learning about the world around them, this made it worth it. This is what gave his life meaning.

Philip had taught this subject over a hundred times and he was still amazed at the range of answers he would find. Sure, some portrayals were standard, like the brooms and pointed hats, but most students had their own ideas about what a witch really was.

"Time," he said at last. The class all looked up from their writings. "Write your names on your papers and turn them in please. You will be happy to know that I am grading these papers on ideas, no matter how far out there they may be. I simply want to relate to you how your ideas and superstitions have all come about. Though we all know there is no such thing as a real witch with magic spells and black cats, this has become a part of our culture, as well as a great many others. I will see you all tomorrow morning, after you have read chapter thirteen, pages 550 to 581."

A groan rose up from the class.

"Good day, people" was all Philip said in reply.

At the same moment that Philip Parker was letting his class go for the day, Captain Kip Gillmore of the Jackson Police Department was walking up to the gates of Parksville Cemetery. He had received the call thirty minutes earlier that the night's extended search for the missing teens had come to its conclusion. An old farmer had happened upon the site. He was so traumatized that Kip had had a hard time understanding him on the phone and now he knew why. In his fifteen years on the force, Kip Gillmore had seen a lot of things, but nothing that could have prepared him for this.

The bodies had remained untouched. The boy, Bud Kennedy, was right where the murderer had left him, hanging naked and exposed. He dangled upside down from the enormous looming oak that stood in the rear of the cemetery and towered above everything else, an old piece of rusty iron rod from the fence thrust through his feet. There was little doubt as to the cause of death, for the boy's throat had been slashed from ear to ear, and the ground below the base of the tree was stained red with his blood.

"It would take two or three good sized men to heave a big strong boy like that up a tree," said Officer Cowan. She was the only woman on the scene and seemed to be handling it much better than most of the menfolk. "I mean, he must be up there a good eight feet. We'll have to wait and see, but my guess is he was alive when they did it. There's no trace of blood anywhere else and no sign of a struggle."

"Hmm," muttered Kip through his thick, black mustache. To look at him, one wouldn't guess he was a cop. He looked more like someone at K-mart Customer Service or a cashier behind the counter at a pharmacy. He never did have that rough-and-tough-guy look about him; yet he was very good at his job, well respected by his men, and when the time came, he could be plenty tough enough.

Kip was taking a mental picture as his eyes canvased the tree and the boy from one end to the other.

"Do you have something in mind sir?"

"Maybe."

Cowan knew better than to press. She had known Kip long enough to know that he kept his views of a case to himself until he was sure. She walked over to where pictures were being taken of young Samantha Hastings and relayed the message to Vinnie who was just slapping another role of film into his camera.

Unlike the young man, Samantha had been left sitting up against a statue of the Virgin Mary some ten feet away. At first glance, one might think her in a quiet slumber, despite her bluish complexion. She seemed at peace, with her head resting softly on one of the statues outstretched arms.

That is, until one looked down to where her mid-section had once been. There was little left from her rib cage to her pelvis except her spine and shreds of dangling flesh. It was as if an enormous creature had walked by and taken a large bite out of her. Still, there was no sign of any struggle.

"I want extra shots of both victims."

Kip took out his notepad and started walking. As he walked, he wrote, his mind working diligently to capture every detail that came to mind. He passed back and forth covering every inch of the cemetery. When he was done investigating, he sauntered through the gates and back to the street, looking, writing, mumbling to himself. Every officer on the Force knew one thing about this part of an investigation: leave the Captain the fuck alone. He didn't want anyone to talk to him, he didn't want anyone asking him any questions, and he didn't want anyone in his way.

"Sam's is going to have his work cut out for him with this one," growled Kip at last, "Cowan, I need a toxicology done on both of them, people don't just let someone do this without some kind of struggle, I want both checked for sexual assault and Cowan . . ."

"Yes, sir?"

"I want that iron rod dusted for prints."

"Vinnie! Where in the fuck is Vinnie?"

"Right here, sir," said Vinnie, leaning on a tree.

"I found some tire tracks coming up the walk way, like someone turned around here, I want those shot for analysis and get me some shots of the gates."

"The gates, but why the . . ." Vinnie started, but then saw the look in Kip's eyes and thought better. He turned and did as instructed.

The rest of the officers stood silent, almost afraid to move.

"The rest of you can stop playing with your dicks and start walking the perimeter, but for God's sake, don't touch anything. Just let me know if you find something."

Instantly, the hive was buzzing as everyone sprang into action.

Kip wiped his brow. Although the heat of the day had yet to set in, he felt warm all over. The vision of people running around in all of the commotion became blurred until nothing remained, except the recollection of himself and Philip Parker standing right here, in this very spot, as they had that day so many years before. They were only ten and more than just friends; they were best friends.

When Kip and his family moved to Parksville, they lived in a trailer park that lay off Union Street in between Parksville and the university. It has since been bought by the university and all the trailers replaced with student housing. Kip was, one might say, from the wrong side of the tracks. Everyone in the park was considered trailer trash and most of the families were single divorcees. Not the right type for that day and age. Kip had lived with his mother and three brothers, all older, and they all stayed pretty much to themselves. That is until the day when Philip came ambling along, kicking a can down the road.

It was summer time and Kip was setting on a blanket in the front yard eating the lunch his mother had prepared before she left for work. With his brothers gone, God knows were, and nothing better to do, he had decided to have a picnic in his front yard. Kip remembered trying to ignore the stranger as he walked by, but that was not the way it happened.

"What you doing eating out here," Phillip asked as he passed.

"Just having a picnic," replied the overly shy Kip.

"Can't have a picnic by yourself, you need a few people to have one."

"Do not," said Kip with a look of fear and defiance in his face

"Look, how about I just sit here with you for a while, that way people won't think you're crazy. I don't want to eat nothing, we can just bullshit until my mom gets done visiting cousin Edna. I hate her trailer, smells like mothballs."

"Sure, why not." Kip relented.

The two hit it off from that day on, even though Philip was from one of the richer families in town, hell the town was named after one of his relatives, he never once acted any better than anyone else.

It had been Philip's idea to come here that day. Even then, he had this thing about studying the past and he had hauled Kip along to search out the oldest remains in Parksville.

"Come on Kippy," Philip had teased, "it'll be bitchin."

Kip, on the other hand had completely different ideas on what was "bitchin," and roaming around in some spooky old graveyard was definitely not one of them. He always gave into Philip sooner or later, and it was late in the day before they had set out. The sun was still bright and the shadows long by the time they had reached the foreboding gates of the cemetery. At first glance, Kip knew he didn't want to go in, but rather than risk being branded a chicken, he did so.

It had not been as bad as he had thought it would be. The cemetery was rather quiet and peaceful. Philip had set right to work at the front of the graveyard reading dates and names, and Kip started to relax once he joined in the search. The ground was covered in shadows by the time they reached the older part of the cemetery and the oak. Here, the headstones were so warn and weathered that nothing legible remained.

"These must have been the first settlers," said Philip with his face aglow. "If so, many of them must have been French trappers and traders."

"Oh, is that ancestor of yours buried here. The one that founded Parksville?"

"Joshua Parker was his name. No, he was buried on his own property, or so they say. Some of these graves might be even older than his. You see this was a traders' camp long before it was ever a town."

"Oh, yeah?" replied Kip unimpressed looking at the rubble spread out around the tree. By this time, the sun was hanging low and a shadow covered the entire ground. "So, I guess we'll never know how old this place really is."

"Nope, I guess not," responded Philip, "the oldest ones are probably not even marked, but one thing's for sure . . ."

"What's that?"

"It's old."

"Well, we'd better get going, don't you think?"

"Yeah, I guess. But man, I sure would like to know who was buried here." Philip closed his eyes and tried to picture what it must have been like when the first white man had come here and the first people were lain to rest.

Kip, just a few feet away had also started to let his imagination run away with him. From every corner of the cemetery he saw the creatures of the night lurking behind trees and stones. Though he couldn't actually see them, he knew they were there, waiting for the night. Unexpectedly, he could hear the wind softly calling him. "Here, I am here. Release me, I implore of thee." Louder and louder came the pleading voice. "Set me free." It was coming from over there, from behind the oak. Without thinking, he began to move forward, toward the voice. Something within him was telling him to resist, but he couldn't help himself. He was no longer in control. It must be set free.

"Well, you ready?" asked Philip.

Kip stopped, dead in his tracks. The spell was broken. For a moment, he stood there, lost in time and space. There was no doubt in his mind that this place, under the oak, did not hold the skeletons of any trappers or New World settlers, but pure evil. He had felt it drawing him nearer to the tree. Felt it pleading with him to dig it loose from its earthly bonds.

Philip walked up from behind him and slapped him on the back, "Hey, I said are you . . ."

Kip screamed and then burst into a mad dash beyond the tree in the direction of the front gates. Just outside, he tripped and fell face down into the dirt. There he stayed, sniveling, until Philip caught up with him and helped him to his feet.

"You okay?" asked Philip gently.

Kip looked up at him. His face was red from fear and shame.

Philip held him close. "It's all right. We all get frightened once in a while."

"Sir."

Kip jumped as he came back to the present. He turned around to see Officer Cowan staring at him. "We're just about done here. Vinnie got the extra shots you wanted. Is there anything else?"

"No," said Kip, still shaking off the memory. "Just make sure that this area is cordoned off and the place is gone over with a fine tooth comb."

"Yes, sir."

"I want those pictures on my desk by noon."

"Yes, sir."

"And Cowan?"

"Yes, sir?"

"Good work," he said then walked away.

Jimmy Martinez walked along the side of the road clad in his filthy flannel shirt and jeans. His chin sported a weird sort of growth that one could not really call a beard because it was patches of hair in no true pattern. He had not bothered to bathe that week and his grimy appearance was almost as disgusting as his odor.

To the town, he simply did not exist, even though most of them passed him every day. It was funny to Jimmy how his chubby body could go unnoticed by everyone; it was like he was invisible, people could see him but chose to look right past.

He had spent most of his life hiking this town and witnessing people doing things that they would never have done in front of descent people, but because he was who he was, people just didn't seem to care. For example, he watched the new teacher at the high school they hired last year take a female student to his house after school. Then he saw them naked through the teacher's bedroom window. He watched Pastor Jacobs at the Baptist Church drinking hard liquor in front of his office window every Sunday after church, has seen the Townson boys shooting up on their way to school; he watched that Professor Parker sit on his front porch and smoke pot; he's seen thirteen-year-old Earl Freeman steal a bottle of wine from the Pop Shop. All this he has seen, and yet no one knows he knows because he is invisible.

Today's mission was to find enough bottles to return, so that he could sneak off and buy a pack of cigs. Mother hated it when she knew he was smoking, but damn it, he was turning thirty this week and he would do what he wanted. Did she always have to treat him like a child? So he was a little slow, (a point she brought up every time she could) he was still a man. Disobeying her was not only fun, it was his way of getting back at her. He had lived under her thumb too long.

A Bud can. All right, he thought reaching down to pick it up. He put it in the black garbage sack he had slung over his shoulder. A few more of these and he would be done be for the day. Then he could go down to the truck stop, hang out with the truckers, and smoke his camels, like a real man.

As he walked, he noticed cop car after cop car coming down the road from the lake, it must have been some accident, he thought. A change in the breeze brushed his dusty cheek, a cool whiff of wind that sent a chill running down his spine. He looked around, something was not right; something had changed. A feeling of loathsomeness overtook him. The air became sour, rotten, filled with the stench of death. He could feel someone or something watching him, peering from the woods. Quickly he turned, crossed the street, and headed back in the direction he had come from. He quickened his pace with every step until he was at a dead run down the side of the road. Finally he stopped, out of breath, sweating like a pig, and looked back. There was nothing there. "Shit," he said aloud to no one. He was done looking for cans today. His heart was pounding in his chest, half from fear and half from exertion. He would go home, take a quick shower and go to the truck stop. There were other ways of making a quick buck, though not at all appealing.

Philip had started to pack all of his lecture notes into his leather brief when Kip, clad in his working grey suit and tie, came walking into his classroom.

"Kip!" said Philip, looking up from his desk with a smile, "What in the hell are you doing here?" He stood up and shook his hand.

"Well, I wish I could say this was a social visit, Phil. But . . ."

"Don't tell me. One of my students?"

"No, not quite, at least I hope not."

Philip looked at Kip with a questioning look on his face.

"Don't worry, you haven't done anything wrong. At least nothing I know about," he said with a smile.

"Well then, why don't you sit down? It's been a long time."

"Yes it has, but if you don't mind, I was wondering if we could go somewhere a little more private to talk."

"Sure, sure, why don't we go to my office?"

"That would be fine."

Phillip got up and made a gesture toward the door.

The halls were all but vacant now. There were no mad rushes to late classes or couples kissing goodbye, just Philip and the overly quiet Kip. As they left the Ford Historical Build and made their way down the path to the main Administration Build and his office, Philip was dying of curiosity.

Philip's office was small but neat. Along every wall there were bookshelves overflowing with wisdom. His desk, far too bulky for the room, sat in front of a large bay window that overlooking the well-groomed campus gardens. Philip offered Kip a seat in the folding chair usually reserved for distressed students, while he himself squeezed behind his desk.

As Philip looked across the desk at his old friend, he was struck by how much the man had changed. Even though they had been close as kids, like many childhood friends, they had drifted apart. After school, Philip had received a free ride at Michigan State then finished his education at P.U. Kip was forced to struggle through the local community college. By the time Philip had returned home with his new wife, Kip had already moved into Jackson. They had tried to stay in touch but neither seemed to have time. It had only been a couple of years since they had seen each other, but Kip seemed different somehow. He was stronger and had a look of confidence that he never had before. Maybe that's what making Captain can do for a man.

Kip rubbed his hand along his cleanly shaven jaw and crossed his legs. He looked deep in thought for a moment as if searching for the right words, then began slowly, "Are you aware that there were two high school kids missing from Parksville?" he asked.

"No, there was nothing on the news."

"Well, we found them, or what was left of them, this morning."

Philip's eyes widened. "Where?"

"Out of town in that old cemetery. You know, that one down by Briskey Lake."

For just an instant Philip thought he saw the older Kip diminish, and in his place sat the frightened little boy that Philip had comforted that day at the cemetery many years ago. It was in his eyes, that same fear. He would never forget that day or the look of terror in Kip's eyes.

"They were both brutally murdered, mutilated. We think they might have fallen prey to," once again Kip considered his words very carefully, "a cult, you know, something Satanic."

"You mean, they were sacrificed?"

"Well, we are not sure."

Philip couldn't believe his ears. It was hard enough to believe a murder of any kind could take place in little old Parksville, but this was more than his mind was able to comprehend.

"Anyway, I have some photos here I want you to look at. Since you are the closest thing we have to an authority on cults, I thought you might be willing to help. Before you say yes, I want to let you know that they won't be easy to look at."

"Okay, I'll give it a shot if it helps."

"You do realize that once you get into this, you're sworn to secrecy. The last thing we need, is some sort of witch hunt going on in Parksville, understand?"

"Yeah, sure."

Kip reached deep into the pocket of his suit coat and pulled out two photos. He handed the first one to Philip. It took some time for Philip to recover from the shock.

The human mind is a strange machine indeed, thought Philip. It was capable of the wonders of Michelangelo and acts as evil as what the picture revealed. Though he had nearly given up on the concepts of God and Satan, he knew good and evil were still alive and well and living in the minds of men. After a couple of minutes, he had prepared himself to look at the other snapshot.

"Well, what do you think? Are we on the right track?"

Philip looked over the desk at Kip. "These pictures make me think that you are right. It looks like the work of a cult. See how the boy is hanging?"

Kip nodded.

"Well, he wasn't just murdered, he was crucified. Crucified upside-down," Philip said almost to himself, "it's a sign of Satan."

"And the girl?"

"There are cults that for centuries have believed in the concept of consuming human flesh. I'm not sure, but to me it looks like someone made a macabre banquet out of her."

Kip hung his head. The same thought had entered his mind. "Well, hopefully we'll know more about that after the coroner's report."

"I see. God, I wish I could be more help, but this isn't a lot to go on." He said as he returned the pictures.

"No, you've been a big help. At least we have an idea of what we are up against, now. If I need you again, I'll get in touch. Remember don't say anything to anyone."

"Sure, no problem. Even if I can't help, I would like to know what happens and I'd really like to stay in touch."

Kip offered him a smile and his hand. "Okay, it's a deal."

By five that evening, Philip was sitting on the porch swing that Elly had insisted on. He had a Bud Light in one hand and a stack of ungraded papers in the other. From here, he could see all of what was left of downtown Parksville. Main Street was lined with six two-story buildings on the right side of the road. The last of which had closed when the new Meijer store opened two years earlier on Interstate 127. The first was the hardware store. He had accompanied his father there many times and they had everything you could imagine in that place: nuts, bolts, nails, screws of every size, any tool you could ever want. Tools for carpentry, tools for farming, tools for plumbing, tools for auto repair. They had it all. Later it was converted into, of all things, an arcade. Next to that was the old drug store with a food counter up front and a pharmacist in back, just as they all used to be. The following two buildings were both clothing stores at one time with one converting to apartments later on. Lastly there was, at one time, the grocery store and the local newspaper. On the left side of the street were Jones's Bar and Grill, Fred's Barber Shop, Millers Feed Store, and the Short Stop Pop Stop, all of them were still open for business.

Beyond were fourteen or fifteen houses, all in need of restoration, then open road that curved to the left, heading for Jackson. If it had not been for the college that sat at the outskirts of Parksville, the town would have been little more than a ghost town. In 1983 the auto industry had left for parts unknown and the college soon became the only resource for making a living. Sure, some drove the ten miles into Jackson looking for work, but everyone knew that it too was dying a slow death, and the only jobs available were unskilled labor at minimum wage. He had seen it all happen from this front porch. Watching as Reagan and his economic reform dried up this peaceful community, bleeding it dry until all that remained were those who lived off the kindness of Uncle Sam, their pride stolen away. If not for the students at Parksville University the entire town may have been entirely forgotten. Though unfashionable, Parksville was convenient for a beer run, night out at the bar, or a cheap haircut.

Philip turned back to his papers. He had just made up his mind to start the tedious job of grading when his neighbor, Bill Smith, came strolling up the small walkway.

Bill was what most people called a hick. He was roughly six-foot-two and must have topped the scales at close to two-eighty. You would always find him in his blue bib overalls and flannel shirt, no matter how hot or cold the weather. Today was no exception. Even though his greatest accomplishment in life had been to graduate from the eighth grade, he was a nice man and a welcome change from all the stuffed shirts at the college.

"Hi teach, what's up?' he asked.

"Not much there Billy Boy, what's up with you?"

"Wife's in one of her moods again. Thought I'd come over and talk to you awhile. You know, 'til she cools off a bit." It was clear he was not in his usual good humor. If anything, he looked like a man that had lost his best friend.

"Have a seat," Philip said making room, "care for a beer?"

"Sure," he said putting on a pained smile and pulling on the straps to his bibs.

Philip smiled and walked into the house. When he returned, Bill was swinging gently back and forth on the swing, his hands buried deep in his pockets. Looking up at Philip, he smiled another sad smile and reached for the beer.

"So, what's Sally pissed off about this time?" asked Philip he really did not want to know, but he figured since he was going to hear it anyway, he might as well get it over with.

"Same old thing," Bill half mumbled and left it at that. He turned his eyes toward town and sighed.

Philip was amazed. Usually this question would have been followed by a cavalcade of complaints. He told her this, and she told him that, and in the end Bill would always tell her what's what and storm out of the house. Philip always suspected that Sally was the one who actually did the telling of what's what but never said so to Bill.

After a few minutes, Bill decided he really did want to tell Philip what was happening. Oh boy, here it comes, Philip thought.

"I'm leaving her," was all Bill said.

"What?" Phillip exclaimed, not trying to hide his surprise. "I'm real sorry to hear that. I knew you two had your problems, but I never realized it had gone that far."

"I hit her," Bill blurted out. "I never thought I could do a thing like that, but I did." His eyes began to tear. "I just can't deal with it. I'm leaving because she deserves better than me."

Philip felt as sorry for him as he had ever felt for anyone.

"I love her so much," Bill said as he wiped his nose on his sleeve, "but she just gets me so fucking crazy that I lost it. I hit her."

Philip watched as this mountain of a man buried his face deep into his pudgy hands and cried openly like a child.

Philip pondered that it is one of mankind's saddest fates that we have forgotten how to comfort. The art of touching, of caring, is often forgotten in the fear of misinterpretation and the sanctity of another's space. Philip wanted to do something, say something, but instead, just stood there and looked at the miserable lost soul in his swing.

After what seemed like an eternity, Bill picked up his beer and finished it off in one long swallow. "I've gotta go."

"You're more than welcome to stay."

"No, I'm sorry to have bothered you with all this, I wasn't planning on saying anything. It just came out."

Philip started to say something, but Bill had made his way off the porch and was heading down the street toward Jones's bar.

Philip felt pity for him, and his heart sank. If only he could have said something, anything. Slowly, he picked up his stack of unmarked papers and tucking them under his arm, headed back into the house.

"Franky," yelled Martha Lake from the bottom of the stairs. "Will you come down here for a moment? There's something I want to talk to you about."

Franky sat on the edge of his brass bed reading a chapter in his English text. "Okay, Mom, be right down." He closed his book with the Garfield bookmark he had gotten at the student bookstore and headed down the hall toward the stairway. "What's up Ma?" he yelled from the top of the stairs.

Mrs. Lake popped around the corner of the kitchen and stared at her only child as he made his way down the last steps. He was a little on the weird side, she had always known that, but in the past six months things had gotten worse. It wasn't the fact that Franky was an underachiever, she and everyone else who knew him could have told you how smart the boy was. The problem with Franky, she hated to say, was that Franky was a nerd. The boy was going on nineteen, had never dated, hung out with friends or even tried to fit in. She knew this isolation was unhealthy for anyone, let alone a young person in their prime.

"I want to talk to you in the kitchen." She gestured toward the round glass table that highlighted the square room.

Franky looked at his mother with a questioning glance. He thought she would most likely have him run down to the Pop Shop or have him feed Boo, the family dog, but now he was at a total loss.

"Coffee?' she asked as he made his way to the table.

"No thanks, that stuff will keep me up all night."

Martha smiled. "Your cousin Jake is going to be staying with us for a while." Her face was becoming firm as she said this. "Now, I know the two of you don't always get along, but he has dropped out of State and has decided to finish out his freshman year this summer at Parksville, so I said he could stay here."

"Mom," grunted Franky, "you know how we get along. He's so fu . . ." he thought better of using the F word in front of his mother, "damn stuck on himself he makes me sick."

"Nevertheless, I've made up my mind. As long as I pay the bills around here, what I say goes. He is my nephew after all, and I can't just leave him out in the street just so it doesn't inconvenience you."

"There's always the dorm," Franky muttered, not quite under his breath.

Martha tightened her face a little more, causing her brow to wrinkle. "Franky, I won't hear any more of this. Now, he gets here Monday, and I want the two of you to get along, so be nice." Her tone changed, the challenging brow relaxed, "Please Franky, for me. Please at least try."

Franky looked at his mother, brushed his long red hair behind his ears and smiled broadly, "okay, for you mom, anything."

"Even if it means being nice to Jake?"

"Even if it means being nice to Jake."

"Thanks honey." She kissed him on the cheek, "I love ya."

Franky got up and left the room, leaving Martha in the kitchen alone. Little did he know that it was actually her idea that Jake finish here, that he was coming at her personal invitation. Maybe Jake's staying there would be a good influence on Franky. After all, Jake was a good looking guy with more than his share of girlfriends. Jake had been popular in Parksville before he and his mother moved to Harrison. Maybe, just maybe, he could teach Franky not to be such a . . . nerd.

Franky sat quietly in his room. Even though large posters of Albert Einstein, John Lennon and J.R.R. Tolkien, hung on his wall, it was his small desk that he turned to now. His desk was overflowing, but it was a framed black-and-white picture of Franky and his father taken just before Frank Sr. died in 1980, that held Franky's attention now. He spent many hours gazing at that picture and even talking to it when he was sure no one else was able to hear. He picked it up and held it level with his eyes. "God, I miss you, Dad." he said and gently returned it to its spot on the desk.

It wasn't that he really hated Jake, he was more jealous of Jake than anything. Franky had been the outcast at school. That's why he had used his sense of humor to survive. He was too tall, too skinny and too damn smart to fit in anywhere. Jake, on the other hand, was captain of the football team, good looking and dumb as a box of rocks. All in all, he was everything a small town girl was looking for. Jake's popularity came naturally to him, the same way Franky's intelligence came to him.

Franky remembered the day when he had won the science fair. The finals had been all the way over in Bridgeman and Martha had taken the day off. She and Aunt Joyce had driven the boys down to the finals. It was to be Franky's day to shine, his day in the spotlight. But when they arrived, Jake had gotten lost downtown and they spent the entire day looking for him. By the time they got to the contest, the names of the winners for his age group had already been given. Though Franky received a trophy on the way out, he had missed his day in the sun, his chance to be the center of attention. The trophy didn't seem very important without the fanfare that went with it.

Martha had tried to make it up to Franky by taking everyone to the beach. She even stopped into a little shop on the way and bought them new swimsuits. But the beach, like the contest, was a letdown. Franky managed to get second degree burns while good old Jake managed to find a girl from Chicago. They disappeared for over a half hour and on the way home, Jake had confided in Franky that he had just lost his virginity at the age of thirteen behind a sand dune. "Right there in broad daylight, in front of God and everybody.

I was so scared someone would see us," he told Franky in a hoarse whisper.

Great, thought Franky, to this day, I have not lost my virginity, and that asshole lost his at thirteen on what should have been my day.

"I hate him," Franky muttered.

The small black and white TV that rested in the corner of the room had begun to flash a pattern by the time Franky completed his homework. His favorite instructor may have been Professor Parker, but his favorite subject was Literature. Their assignment had been easy enough, write a poem, any kind of poem, only it had to deal with an unpleasant subject matter yet pleasing to the ear of the reader. He looked down at what he wrote.

The Rose

I saw the boy as he sat in anguish along the pier, eyes red and sore from the steady stream of tears that glistened upon his young handsome face. For all these tears one's heart must be torn and so I spoke unto the lad, "Is a lover gone with the wind worth this self-inflected torture, can not a heart be born in love again and blossom as a rose in spring?

He turned his eyes to meet my own and through broken speech he uttered back unto me, "And how long can a rose in full bloom exist without the essence of spring and summer, when the sun has traveled far away and with it the warmth on which the rose must feed?

I was lost for words that would spark hope unto the lad. Throughout the night he kept his silent vigil along the pier, watching timeless waves going nowhere.

I woke with the morning sun and glancing from my cabin door I noticed the boy had vanished. Though my eyes searched the docks and landings, he was not to be found. Then, perchance, I glanced solemnly out to sea and there I saw riding atop the waves a rose. I knew its very meaning, its truest meaning, and my very soul felt pain.

What a work of shit, he thought and closed his notebook. He turned off the TV and lay down on his bed, thoughts of Sue Barkley filtering into his brain. She was so lovely, smart, and kind that Franky had fallen hopelessly in love with her. He lay on his Garfield comforter clad only in his boxer shorts and a pair of socks that did not match. His hand made its way down to his swollen manhood and he began rubbing it. Slowly he let his fingers glide over the small titillated bumps of its head. Then he began to gently stroke the shaft, slowly at first, then harder and quicker as visions of Sue Barley, lying on the bed next to him became more erotic. Soon he was lost in a world of sexual fantasies and physical pleasure. Suddenly, there was a knock on his door.

"You had better call it a night Franky. You've got class in the morning," Martha said from behind the door. "You know how hard it is to get you up in the morning."

Franky opened his eyes, the visions were gone in a flash. "Yeah Mom. I'm going to turn in right now." Thank God she never came in uninvited.

"All right, good night."

"Night Mom." Franky answered. With that, he lay back on his bed, the mood gone for at least this evening. If only there were some way to get Sue to like him, he thought, reaching over to shut off the lamp near his bed.

When closing time had come to Jones's Bar and Grill, Bill had managed to go through a third of his last pay check, which he had picked up, along with his lay-off notice, earlier that day. Even the college was having its problems it appeared, and even though Bill had worked as a custodian there for five years, he too was feeling the effect.

He gazed around the now empty bar, the pennants of college teams, pro-teams, and the regional high schools adorned the walls. Glass mirrors with Budweiser, Miller, and Michelob were scattered here and there. The two pool tables sat well-lit but quiet; there was no loud clanking of balls. The large Wurlitzer jukebox at the end of the bar had just finished playing a country song that he didn't know, something about having fun on the bayou, and now it too stood silent. Alone, he felt so alone.

When he told Sally that he was laid off, she flew into a fit of rage. "You worthless piece of shit. You ain't got nothing going for you. Why I stayed with your fat ass this long is beyond me. I could have married any man in this town. But no, I had to link up with a good for nothing like you. What the hell are we gonna do about the fucking bills, now. Any brilliant fucking ideas?"

Bill looked into Sally's immense green eyes, he knew she was right. She probably could have had any man in town. To say she was pretty was an understatement. She had the body of a goddess and that natural beauty seldom found in any woman. However, getting and keeping a man were two different things and along with her looks came her temper and selfish attitude that any other man would have told her to stick up her ass a long time ago.

"Answer me," she screamed and reached out to claw him with her long painted nails. She never got the chance. Bill had nailed her with a good backhand that dropped her like a stone. She had taken her claws to him before and he carried the scars to prove it.

"Come on Bill, let's call it a night."

Bill looked up and saw Ken Jones starring down at him. Ken ran the bar by himself since his wife had passed on and by closing time, he was more than ready to crawl up to his apartment and finish off at least a six-pack by himself.

"It's 2:30 and I want to get the hell out of here."

Bill just glared back with drunken eyes. Slowly he moved his large frame down from his stool.

"Remember what I said. I could always use an extra guy behind the bar." Actually, Ken was not telling the truth. He had run the bar by himself for so long that anyone else back there would have only been in the way. But he had known Bill since he was a kid and his father had been a good customer before him. He had a heart of gold, but would deny it to the bitter end, instead liking people to believe with his stone-face that he was as cold as he pretended to be. Ken was the only one who ever thought the charade worked.

Bill just waddled toward the door, not bothering to answer. He did not want charity, even when he was so drunk he couldn't give you the meaning of the word.

"Poor bastard," Ken muttered. He went to chase the rest of the late night locals out of the bar.

Outside, the cool night air bit into Bill's face. It felt good on his burning cheeks. He looked left for a while and then right, not knowing where it was he wanted to go or what he wanted to do. Finally, he headed further up Main Street and out of town, swaying from side to side with every step he managed.

About a mile out of town Bill began to recover slightly. His head was still swirling, but his legs had managed to stiffen a little, which improved his walking.

"Bitch! Stupid bitch," he screamed at the top of his lungs. "I should go back there and wring her pretty little neck." His head began to swirl more as he yelled, "Why did I have to go and hit her? I love her. She is a bitch but God help me, I do love her." without a pause, he began to cry loud, full sobs from deep in his chest. He looked around, lost and bewildered. "Got to get my shit together," he spoke to the empty night, "got to sober up and go home. Worst she could do is kill me, right? Wait behind the door with a butcher knife and get me in the back, right?"

Conflicting emotions of love and hate began tearing him apart: "Gotta get myself together. Besides, I can't sleep out here in the middle of nowhere can I? I ain't no goddamn hobo am I? Anyway, it's my fucking house. It was the sweat off my balls that paid for that fucking house. If she doesn't like it, just get out baby." He began to laugh as hard as he had been crying just a few minutes ago. If anyone had been driving down Main Street that night, they would have no doubt that the large man standing in the middle of the road, laughing up at the stars, had gone stark raving mad.

The laughter slowly died, however, and again the tears came. Quietly this time, "Got to sober up, got to go back and tell her I love her."

With this now being his only thought, he turned off Main St. and started down Railroad Street. There were only a few summer houses on the lake and in his disoriented state of mind, Briskey Lake was as good as anywhere to sober up and think things through. More than once, he had taken a quick dip in order to sober up before he faced Sally. Maybe that was the reason he headed that way in the first place. Maybe he knew all along what he was going to do. Maybe he even had things already figured out and just didn't know it yet.

It was a half-mile walk to the lake down the old tracks. When he got to the Yorkey's cottage he began to undress on their back porch. The Yorkeys lived in Florida all winter and came up here only after the first of June. Bill was sure no one would see him. After removing his clothes, he walked around to the front of the house. The lake was calm and the moonbeams shone like glass on its surface. Across the lake was the Richardson place, they lived in Virginia, then the Gibson place. The Gibsons were both retired and sure to be in bed at this time of the night. At the far right, stood the remains of the old manor. No one had lived there for over a hundred years, or so the story goes. The cool night air had kept away the high school and college kids who often came down here for a quick piece or to get off skinny dipping. It was here, in this very spot, that he first felt the scrape of Sally's nails running down the length of his back. God, they were so young then.

Bill walked up to the water's edge and tested it with his big toe. It was cold. The first of April in Michigan was no time to be thinking about swimming, but the cold was just what Bill thought he needed. He began walking slowly out into the dark water, dreading the moment when the water would reach his groin. When it did he felt pain rush all the way through him, but it only lasted a second. Reluctantly he splashed water over his head and down his back. The cold cut like a knife but he welcomed it, feeling more and more awake, feeling a little more sober. He needed to be awake and sober to face the ordeal ahead of him. When the water finally reached his neck, Bill took a deep dive. He came out of the water gasping for warm air and pushed the wet hair out of his eyes. In the moonlight, he saw something sticking out of the water directly in front of him only a few feet away. There was just enough of it visible. His first thought was to swim out to see what it was, but before he got the chance, it simply sank under the water. "Damn," muttered Bill. He felt an urge suddenly to get away from there. He was sober enough now and he had a bad feeling in his gut. He turned toward shore, but then it happened. A dark shape came flying out of the water just inches from his nose. It took a moment for his eyes to focus on what it was and then he began to scream.

It was an arm, long and white, with skin hanging in tatters from the bone. The claw that protruded from the end was curled with long, black pointed nails. He tried to move, but never got the chance. It came crashing down on his head with a loud plop. Surging pain rushed through his brain. Quickly, he raised his mammoth arms trying to break it loose, but the nails kept digging deeper into his scalp. Bill began pounding at it with his huge fist only to feel the grip tighten. His last thought was of Sally's long painted nails, then he was pulled under the water to the waiting creature below. The lake churned with violent motion and then was colored red with Bills blood. Then as suddenly as it started, it was over. The lake was still again and the moon shone on the surface like glass.

FRIDAY

Sally Smith reached over to the empty space her husband usually occupied on the other side of the bed. She gently ran her hand over the silk sheet as if she were caressing his large body. He had finally done it, left her. She always knew that he would leave. After all, how long could any man put up with her abuse. She had driven him off so many times only to wake up and see his loving face looking back at her in the morning. Well, not this time. This time, she had gone too far and he was not going to come back. It was her fault that he had hit her, she knew that even at the time. Now she was alone, and every mean and evil thing she had done or said to that sweet teddy bear of a husband came back to her in a blinding flash. Every cruel word, every wicked insult, came crashing home. She had made his life a living hell since that long ago lovely day he had slipped that modest gold band over her finger. So, this is how it ends, she thought, without a good bye, without even a last kiss.

She hugged his pillow to her face and lost the fight in her attempt to keep from crying. She could call her mother for comfort, but she doubted there would be much forthcoming from that direction. Her mother had warned her that if she didn't control that temper and mouth of hers, this is exactly what would happen. The last thing she wanted to hear right now was, *I told you so*. Finally, she got out of bed and headed across the bedroom, her long satin nightgown softly sweeping the hardwood floor.

In the mirror, the red blotch below the left eye had swelled and darkened to a deep purple. "Shit," said Sally to her reflection in the mirror, "he nailed me a good one." She smiled in spite of the pain, not because he had hit her, there was no excuse for that, but because, for the first time since she had known him he had actually stood up to her. She had always been able to run his life according to her own whim; she had always been in control. She remembered that time in Jones's bar when she had reached out and dug him so deep with her nails that it left two thin scars on his face, all because he had been sitting with good for nothing Tina Tucker when Sally walked in. He just sat there and took it, didn't even raise a hand to defend himself. Later that night, in a calm but firm voice, he told her, "You will never do that to me again." She passed it off as she had almost everything he said that did not fit into her life's plan. Now she wished she had listened to him. There was just so much any man could take.

Suddenly her face lit up with a new realization and her mood changed, from misery to total exhilaration. Princess was barking for her morning meal from somewhere in the back yard. He may leave what little clothes he had, or his old beat up '76 Grand Prix, but he would never leave that damn dog. Princess was his pride and joy. He had saved for months to buy the full-blooded golden retriever and had loved it as if it were his only child. She had really jumped in his face about spending the money on that mutt, but now that same mutt was going to get her husband back. She just knew it.

Sally flew to the large bi-fold doors that opened into the large walk-in closet of the bedroom. It was filled almost entirely with her clothes, less than a foot was reserved for Bill's five flannel shirts, his three pair of Wrangler jeans and of course his spare pair of bibs. The rest of his clothes she had sold, at what was advertised as the first garage sale of the year. Parksville was known for its garage sales. By selling all his old clothes, when winter came and he needed a new wardrobe, she would insist on getting one too. It was only fair. It was not that she needed a new wardrobe, almost all of Bill's hard earned money went into her wardrobe, but if she couldn't be the richest woman in Parksville, she could damn well dress the part.

She rooted through her garments like a woman searching for her lost child in a crowd. Suddenly, she stopped and looked in awe at what she beheld. The red dress she had bought at Gabrielle, the malls most expensive shop. It was made of the finest silk. Swiftly she pulled it from the hanger and rushed back to the bathroom.

After twenty minutes she appeared like a vision. Her face was painted to perfection. Her eye shadow was a light emerald color that highlighted her bright, beautiful green eyes. Her lips were a sensuous red, and the cover stick she had used on the bruise had almost done the trick with only a small, purple spot remaining right at the edge of her eye. Her dress fit to perfection, as did all of her clothes. It came to the upper part of the knee exposing her long, shapely legs. The top was low-cut showing, a dangerous amount of cleavage and the back was completely open until it reached the small of her back just above the buttocks.

Sally walked around to the back of the house and peered out the back porch window. Princess was still there, lying under an old willow tree, panting. When she saw Sally appear at the window the dog immediately started to bark to inform Sally that she was still waiting to be fed. Sally smiled at the mutt and ran into the kitchen where she poured an overly generous portion of dog food into one of her grandmother's best china bowls. She then filled another bowl with water and went outside to feed her best friend.

Back inside she sat silently by the front window waiting for Bill to walk across the front porch. She did not have to watch, she had become accustomed to the sound only his large feet could make on the loose boards of the porch; she would just sit here and wait.

What if he just walked around back without coming in? The thought alarmed her. Her first impulse was to wait on the porch sofa, but she quickly changed her mind. What would the neighbors say, her sitting out on the front porch at seven in the morning dressed like a hooker in a B movie? Instead, she pulled the curtains way back and moved her rocker in such a way that she could see the entire street from where she sat.

She had it all figured out. When he got home she would talk him into going down to Jones's for lunch. She would tell him what a fool she had been, that it was her fault he had hit her, that she would never try to claw him again. Yes, she would tell him all these things and then they would come home and make love. She would do the things to him he had always wanted her to do, all the things he had longed for her to do, anything that would bring him back for good.

In the early morning light she sat, silently waiting for that familiar shape to make his way up Main Street.

Philip arrived for only the last fifteen minutes of his eight o'clock class. He had overslept. In all the years he had been teaching, he had never overslept, but this morning he had reached over, shut the alarm off and gone back to sleep. For the second night in a row he had been bothered by nightmares, and last night he awoke and spent much of his night staring into the darkness of an empty room, afraid of falling back to sleep and back into the terror. Again, this morning there was no memory of his dreams' content, but the fear remained.

The only students who had waited for him were Franky and Sue. They were both sitting on the front of his desk chatting about the cruel fate that must have befallen their favorite teacher. The thought of him simply over sleeping had never once crossed either of their minds. Professor Parker simply would never do such a thing. Something terrible must have happened, that was the only logical answer. He must have fallen down the stairs, had a heart attack, or something every bit as dramatic because the man had never missed a class, and he was never, ever, late.

Philip smirked as he walked in causing both students to jump off his desk like they had just been caught playing doctor in the hall closet. "Sorry guys, I overslept."

Both looked at him in disbelief.

"Come on," Philip laughed, "I am human you know."

"Sorry," Sue said in a timid voice, "It's just not like you to miss class, we were afraid something had happened."

"I know," he agreed and scratched his head as if to relate his own bewilderment at the situation. "Thank God it's Friday."

"Thank God," Sue said.

"Thank God," Franky echoed.

"How about I spring for coffee in the cafeteria? It's the least I can do."

"Sure," came the joint reply.

"We will have to go over to the one in Jefferson Hall, all the others are closed today," said Franky.

Phillip gave Franky a quizzical look as to why they were closed.

"I love that place," spouted Sue.

"Great," Philip responded. He wondered how the rest of the class would respond to his truancy come Monday. He would most likely get ribbed by his overzealous class. "Well then, let's move it out," he said and gestured toward the door.

The cafeteria in Jefferson Hall was unconventional in the fact it only served coffee and bagels. Everything else, including hamburgers and hot dogs, came from vending machines. Even though it was a hive of activity during the winter months, increasingly warm weather had been luring the students out, so Philip didn't think much about it being nearly empty.

"Well, at least you picked a good day to come in late, "Sue teased from behind her steaming cup of coffee.

"Yeah," Franky laughed, but his eyes never left Sue.

"What do you mean?" asked Philip.

"Only half the class showed up today anyway," Sue answered.

"Everyone was trying to get an early start I guess," Franky said, pulling his hair back behind one ear.

"What in the world are you two talking about?" Philip questioned in a bewildered tone.

"Why, spring break, of course." Sue's face had filled with concern as she answered. "You know, two whole weeks away from good old P.U. How could you forget that?"

Philip laughed, "I don't know, it honestly slipped my mind. Damn, I can't believe I forgot."

"Have you been feeling all right Dr. Parker?" Sue asked, the look of concern planted on her face.

"Yes, fine." he smiled to set her mind at ease. "I've been having a hard time sleeping the past few nights is all."

Franky gave him a questioning glance.

"Maybe I'm still half asleep, I don't know. So, what are you going to do over spring break?" he added in an obvious attempt to change the subject.

Franky, who was still looking oddly at Philip, as if to have more clarification, started to speak, but for the life of him could not figure out what to say. Besides, he was far more interested in what Sue was doing over spring break.

"Well, one thing I am not going to do is go back to Chicago," Sue stated emphatically, "in fact, I was thinking of moving out of the dorm and finding a place in Parksville."

"Parksville?" Philip asked in amazement. "Why Parksville?"

"Why not?" Sue shot back.

"Well, I just thought a big city girl such as yourself would prefer a faster pace, something at least as big as Jackson."

"No way, I'm in the market for a little peace and quiet."

"I'll help you," Franky blurted out, "find a place to live I mean. I live in Parksville."

Sue turned to Franky and smiled, "Thanks, it would help to have someone who knows the area." Actually, Sue thought Franky was nice, he always acted like a gentleman, and she imagined that somewhere under all that hair, he might even be somewhat cute.

"Well, if you need help moving, give me a call," Philip offered, "but I still don't think you'll like it there. There's not much going on, and we roll up the sidewalks at ten o'clock."

Franky gave Philip another strange look, he had lived in Parksville all his life and while he agreed that it was definitely not the liveliest of places, he had always liked living there.

"That is just what I want." Sue answered. She leaned back a little in her chair and crossed her legs. In doing so, she exposed her long tan legs through the slit in her already too tight skirt. Philip didn't seem to notice, but Franky felt warm all over and was sure his face was turning a bright red. "I still have two wonderful months until I graduate and then I thought I would take the summer off and relax. I have already cleared it with my folks. In fact, they are behind me one hundred percent. It's a cheaper graduation present than sending me to Europe which is what I wanted in the first place."

Now, Franky was truly amazed at what he'd heard. Here he and his mother had been struggling to get him through college and Sue was getting an extra summer out of state for a graduation present, all expenses paid. And why in the world would anyone give up a chance to go to Europe to stay in Parksville? But curiosity gave way to the realization that soon Sue would be spending the entire summer so close. And, the only ones she would know in the area were Professor Parker and himself. This might turn out to be the best summer of his life.

Philip looked up at the clock that hung above the cafeteria's front door: five minutes to nine. "Well, I have to go,' he said, "I can't be late for another one."

"So do I," Franky said, and the two men got up and left together, leaving Sue alone at the small round table.

"Besides," sighed Sue after they were both out of hearing range, "I'll be closer to you, Professor Parker."

Martha Lake hung the week's laundry on the line her husband had put up over ten years earlier. It was turning out to be a nice, warm day, and she wanted to get that fresh smell that only open air could put into her clothes. Over her back fence, she saw the Smith's dog, Princess attacking a bowl of dog food. Those are pretty nice bowls to be using for dog dishes, she thought to herself. But then again, the Smiths were not your average couple. She had spent many a long, sleepless night listening to their fighting from her bedroom window. As a matter of fact, it was always Sally she heard, never Bill.

The Lake's house was on Maplewood, which lived up to its name for it was lined with long rows of maple trees. The houses on this street, like those on Main, were mostly in need of paint, some new siding and general maintenance. The Lake's house was no exception. She worked hard at the loan office to keep the place up but with Franky at P.U., the bills had really started to pile up. There just wasn't enough to go around. She knew that if her husband had lived, they would have been able to move from the older part of town to the new subdivision just off Chestnut Street.

There, the houses were all split level jobs with a few ranches thrown in. Once, Franky Senior had even talked about buying that empty lot on Briskey Lake where the old manor rested. "We could build a lovely little cottage for just the three of us." That is just what he said, and if he had put his mind to it, no doubt it is just what he would have done.

From inside the house, the telephone began to ring. It was probably her work calling. She had planned to take her floating holidays on Friday and Monday so that she might enjoy a four-day vacation. Every time she took one of her floating holidays, she could expect at least one call asking her where this file was, what the new access code was, or something equally unimportant. She set the wicker basket down and ran inside.

Kip Gillmore was having a miserable day. The entire afternoon was spent talking to the kids at Parksville High. He had turned up nothing. If the two murdered kids did have any link to a cult, they were either the only ones who knew it or everyone was doing a brilliant job of covering it up.

Kip sat at the May Day Diner, a quaint little restaurant in the heart of Jackson, awaiting the arrival of Father McMurry. He had made the appointment for three o'clock earlier in the day and now wished he hadn't. The good Father was already twenty minutes late and Kip had already ordered and eaten. He doubted the priest could shed much light on the subject anyway. Still, dealing with some kind of Satan worship, it seems only natural to speak to someone from the Church.

Kip looked around the busy cafe. It was rather serene here and no one seemed to be in a hurry. The walls were all painted white with depictions of clowns on black velvet hanging every ten feet. Not a place for an art critic, but a decent place to take the family and grab a bite to eat. Bright and cheerful were the words you could use to describe it. In the mad rush of the city, it was always nice to have that one place where you could go and leave the city, with its clamor and movement outside. More than once, he had considered moving back to the slow pace of Parksville, but the city, whether or not he liked it, was now his home. If he had married, maybe it would be different, but he didn't think so. The city was now in his blood.

An old man outfitted in black came strolling through the front door. Kip saw the collar and waved him over. It was no surprise the man was late, he looked like he was a hundred years old. "Well, hello there young feller," said the priest offering his hand, "I'm Father McMurry."

"Hello," replied Kip. As the two shook hands, Kip was surprised by how strong his grip was. "Captain Gillmore, JPD."

"Sorry to be late," said the priest as he sat down, "I got stuck helping the seventh grade with their backstrokes."

"Really," responded Kip trying to hold back a chuckle.

"Yep, they think that because I'm older than dirt they can lick me. I whooped their asses by a country mile." He grinned.

Whatever his first impression may have been about the good Father, it was clear that he was letting no grass grow under his feet. He appeared full of life and vigor, almost bouncy in a way. Still, being a good Baptist, Kip didn't have any idea how one went about striking up a conversation with a Catholic priest. As it turned out, it was never a problem because McMurry took the lead.

"So, what can I help you with?" He was not shy and went straight to the point, an admirable attribute in Kip's book.

"There's been a murder in Parksville."

"So I've heard," answered the priest.

"We think it has something to do with a satanic cult."

"And you were wondering if I, being a man of the cloth, might have some insight."

"Yeah, that's about it," Kip admitted.

"Well Mr. Fillmore . . ."

"That's Gillmore, Father."

"Right, Gillmore. You're not Catholic are you?"

"No Father, I'm not."

"Too bad," joked McMurry. "Anyway, I wish I could be of some help, but you see, I know very little about such matters. I chase a far more dangerous field. I'm an educator."

Kip offered the man a hearty smile.

"You know though, come to think of it, I may have something that may be of interest. I don't know if it will help but I have an old manuscript from the Priest who founded St. Timothy's. It deals with a case back in the early eighteen hundreds."

"Well, I don't see how . . ."

"Now wait a minute, this case was about a man that tried to start a cult in Parksville, or whatever the hell it was called then. The story was rather bizarre. I think I remember reading it when I first got here, must have been what, fifty years ago. There was this old book that went along with it. I'm sure it's stuck up there in the archives somewhere."

"Could I possibly have a look at it?" Kip asked. He still doubted it could be connected to the crime but who knows. Maybe this cult had been underground all these years or maybe these kids found a similar copy and were trying to bring back some ancient cult. It was a long shot, a real long shot, but for now it was as good as anything else he had to go on.

"Well, the transcript will be of little use to you . . . unless you happen to speak perfect Latin."

"That I cannot do."

"As for the book, it seems there is some kind of restriction on its use. The Church has some materials the public isn't allowed to see. Why don't I have another look at it and tell you if I find anything you might find of interest."

"Sure, why not."

"Have you eaten?"

"Yes, I'm sorry but I ate while I was waiting."

"Good, how about we go over to Kellys for a beer then."

"I'm on duty."

"So am I, but I won't tell if you don't."

As the sun went down, it left a canvas brightly painted in shades of orange and purple. Spring had come early this year and the warm breeze lightly brushed Sue Barkley's long golden hair back as she stood alone in the open doorway of the Jackson's Mall Twin Theaters. She stopped for a moment, letting the touch of spring caress her face with the softest of touches. The movie *Moonstruck* was everything she heard at the dorm, romantic, funny, and more. It had left her feeling romantic, wishing it had been Professor Parker instead of some old man sitting next to her during those funny yet tender moments in the theater. Slowly she strolled to her car; she lifted her spring jacket, waving it back and forth in front of her, making it dance to a quiet version of That's Amore. She looked into the sky; the moon had just begun to come out. She sighed. When she reached her car, she threw the jacket into the open window, a romantic night like this should not go to waste. She hopped into her Firebird and headed for the nearby park. She had been dreaming about a nice walk there, not alone of course but with Professor Parker. They would find a discreet place and walk together, hand in hand, whispering quiet sweet nothings to each other like lovers do. When darkness came he would take her in his strong arms and begin to kiss her on the shoulder and neck. Then, when she began to quiver he would finally kiss her lips, gently at first, then becoming more demanding, biting her ever so gently. He would move his hands slowly over her body, places where a nice girl would have objected to being touched. Then she let out a sigh.

The park was completely empty. The rows of benches that lined its paths, each bench under its own lamp, gave her the impression of a thousand lovers, all of whom had sat there at one time or another, gazing into each other's eyes. She could almost see them as they sat, holding each other in their arms. She could see herself sitting there, Parker's arm around her. "Someday," she spoke in a soft voice. "Someday."

From across the road, Franky watched Sue's every move. He had been there at the movie, just six rows back. As a matter of fact, he had only been a stone's throw away from her since she had left campus that afternoon. He had followed her to the dorm and waited patiently until she came out. He had watched from a far booth while she ate her dinner at Pizza Hut, and even shadowed her as she made her way through every lady's shop at the mall. She had not spotted him, he was sure of that. If she had seen him, he would have acted like it was just a coincidence. He would have told her it was his mother's birthday and he was shopping for a gift. He watched now as she made her way down the path that divided the park in half. The trees had not started to bud yet and it was easy to see her in the moonlight.

He wished he had the nerve just to walk over and start up a conversation. Even to say hello would have been enough to satisfy him at this point. But he couldn't, for now he would have to be content to just watch.

Philip arrived home after dark. He had spent the evening with a fellow professor from the social science department. He had more than his limit of three beers and was feeling good. As he made his way up Main, he noticed a commotion in front of the Smith house. There were two police cars and an ambulance, all three with their lights going, parked in the driveway. He quickly parked his MG in his own drive and got out to see what was going on. The first person he saw was Martha Lake. She was walking around the corner and heading down Mill Street, which ran between his house and the Smith's.

"Mrs. Lake," Philip yelled.

Martha turned, "Oh, it's you, Mr. Parker." She made her way across the road and up to his front lawn where he stood waiting.

"What's wrong at the Smith's?" He asked when she got close enough to carry on a conversation.

"It's Sally," she said.

Just then the front door of the Smith's house burst open and out came three men dressed in blue carrying a stretcher. Sally Smith, strapped into place, was throwing her head back and forth, her eyes red and glassy.

"She tried to commit suicide," Martha continued with her head slightly bowed.

"Suicide?" Philip could hardly believe it. Sally had always been the strong one in that family. Besides she was so self-centered, it was hard to imagine her doing bodily harm to herself.

"Well, that's what they think anyway." Martha answered.

"Poor girl." Philip turned to Martha. She was shaking all over. "Would you like to come in for a cup of tea Mrs. Lake? It may help you relax a little bit."

Martha smiled. She hadn't realized her discomfort was so apparent. "Yes, I think that would be nice."

Once inside Philip's small kitchen, Martha began to feel better. Philip put on the kettle and then made his way to the chair across the table from where she sat.

"Were you the one who found her?' he asked, gently.

"Well, you know how that air head mailman, Eddie, is always screwing up the mail. This was the third time this week I got someone else's. Luckily, this time it was Sally's. When I went over there to give it to her, no one came to the door. I was going to leave when I saw her just sitting there in front of their big bay window. Her eyes, they had this faraway look. I knew right then that there was something wrong, so I walked right inside and well . . ."

"Do you know what she took?"

"There was a half-empty bottle of Valium sitting right next to her. The first thing I did was take her into the kitchen and stick my finger down her throat to make her vomit. While she was throwing up in the sink, I called 911."

"Well, I think you did a wonderful job. A lot of people would have just walked away when they saw her sitting there all spaced out."

The kettle on the stove began to screech.

"Excuse me," said Philip as he got up to silence the kettle and pour the tea. As he stood over the two cups, waiting for the bags to produce that desired shade of brown, his head swirled with questions. He could see that Mrs. Lake was upset from reliving the experience, so he decided not to pursue the line of questioning just now. He was at a loss about what else they could discuss. Even though they were neighbors, he had only really met the lady once. It was last year, during the Parksville Celebration. They had closed off the street for a parade, fireworks, games and a host of flea markets. It was the first time the two had ever set eyes on each other. Franky and his mother were standing in his front yard watching the parade when Philip had come out and sat on the porch swing. At once, Franky walked over and introduced himself. Philip had seen the boy in the neighborhood before. Franky announced he would be going to P.U. in the fall and had signed up for one of his classes. Then he yelled at his mother and introduced the two as if he had known Philip all his life. Since then, he had seen her and nodded or said hello but that had been the extent of it.

"Did you know that Bill had left her?" he finally asked.

"No, I didn't know that."

"At least that's what he told me yesterday."

"Well, I'm sorry to hear that," she said. Actually, it came as no big surprise, but she didn't say so to Philip.

Philip finished with the tea and walked back over to the table.

"Strange times have come to Parksville," said Martha.

"Sugar or cream?" asked Philip handing her the cup.

"This is fine, thank you."

"What do you mean by strange times?" he asked, picking up the conversation.

"Didn't you hear? It was all over the six o'clock news."

"No. I stayed in town for dinner and haven't had a chance to catch the news yet."

"Well, you know they found those kids yesterday?"

"Yes, I heard."

"They found them down at that old cemetery, murdered. Now they're saying it might have been a cult thing. Can you believe it?"

Philip did his best to act surprised, the voice of Kip ringing in her ears, "You can't tell anyone about this."

"And now this," she said looking deep into her cup.

Again, Philip's mind filled with a million uninvited questions. Had Kip made a statement to the press? Had his name been used? He suppressed his questions again. All he needed to know would be re-broadcasted at eleven. Until then, he would just have to wait.

"Well, enough of this gloomy talk," Martha said. She too was trying to change the subject and Philip was all for it. "How is Franky doing in your class?"

"Well, Mrs. Lake . . ."

"Please call me Martha."

"O.K. Martha. Well to be quite honest with you I think Franky is one of the brightest students I've had in years. I really have to stay on my toes with that one."

Martha did not look or act at all surprised by that piece of information. "He really is a good boy. I was afraid he might run wild after his dad passed on, but he has never given me a minute of trouble. You might think it's strange, but in a way I almost wish he had."

"Now, that's something you don't hear every day. A mother wishing her son was a problem child."

"Oh, I don't mean real trouble," she said embarrassed at her own openness. "I'm not saying I want him involved in drugs or gangs, just the kind of trouble young men his age get into when they are having a good time."

Philip gave her a questioning look.

"I was young once myself Mr. Parker."

"Philip, please."

"I'm sorry, Philip, anyway, like I said I was young once myself, and I know that having fun at that age does not always mean keeping your nose clean."

Philip was truly impressed with her honesty. In fact, he was impressed with everything about her.

"Have you ever been married Philip?"

The question had obviously taken him by surprise and it showed on his face.

"I hope you don't mind my asking, but you are a very good-looking man and around here, you must be quite a catch."

Philip laughed in spite of himself.

"No, I mean it. All the girls at our breakfast club have their eyes on you."

"Well, there's no accounting for taste," he said. "And to answer the question and soothe their curiosity, yes. I was married, my wife was killed in a car accident some years ago."

"I'm sorry." Martha was feeling about an inch high.

"It's okay, really."

"Well, I really am sorry."

"I'm sure you know what it's like. You're a widow aren't you?"

"Yes, and I know it's not easy. I didn't date for the longest time."

"I still don't," said Philip as he raised his cup and emptied it. Looking over at Martha, he noticed that her cup was empty too. "Would you like another one?"

"Yes, I believe I would."

"Great," he got up and put the kettle back on to boil. "Can I ask you something, Martha?"

He wasn't sure why, but he felt as if he could talk to her as he hadn't been able to talk to anyone else since Elly died. Maybe it was because she had lost someone too that made him so comfortable with her.

"Sure, what is it?"

"Why is it that some people take so long before they are ready to be with someone else when they lose the person they love? Other people seem to be able to pull it together and get back to the business of living. I mean it was so long ago, but I still . . ."

"Maybe it's because you are trying to find a carbon copy."

"Do you think so?"

"Well, I'm not an expert, but with me it was as if I had built a god-complex around Frank Senior. It was like I could never be happy with a man that was not exactly like him. Of course, I thought he was perfect in every way, when they're gone, it is easy to forget all the little things, like picking his teeth at the dinner table or the way his feet stank. All those things get blocked out because you don't want to remember anything bad about them. When you put someone that high up on a pedestal, it is impossible for anyone else to reach your standards. I'm not saying Frank was not a wonderful man, because he was and I loved him with all my heart, but he was not a saint. I know that I will always love Frank, but it's time for me to be happy, too. That's what he would have wanted. And if I do fall in love again, it won't make me love him any less. It may not be the same, but it may be wonderful in its own way. Do you know what I mean?"

"So, why haven't you remarried?"

Martha burst out laughing. "Because dating, and marriages are two different things."

"I guess you're right," Philip laughed.

"I may remarry one of these days, after Franky moves out, and if I were to meet someone I cared for enough."

Philip was looking at Martha, her body did not show its forty years and her eyes were gentle and caring. He felt something stir inside himself, something he had not felt for a very long time.

The kettle interrupted his line of thinking by shrilling its ear-piercing song.

For the next two hours, they sat and talked. They talked about friends they shared, their lives in Parksville, about the past and of course they talked more about Frank and Elly. Together, they shared the joys and heartaches of being with someone they loved. When Martha finally looked up at the clock over the stove, she was surprised to see they had been talking for so long. "Oh my goodness, look at the time. I've got to get going. Franky will be worried to death." Philip walked her to the door. "Thank you for everything; you are a very nice man."

"No, thank you. You have helped me more tonight than you can ever imagine."

Martha turned from the open door, "Please stop over sometime and I can make you some tea to return the favor."

"I would like to do that but do you know what I would like even more?"

"Coffee," joked Martha.

"No" smiled Philip "I just thought that maybe . . ."

Martha tilted her head slightly and smiled a coy smile. "Are you asking me out on a date Professor Parker?"

"Why yes Mrs. Lake, I do believe I am."

"You'll be sorry, I'm a very big eater," Martha teased.

"That's okay, they pay us Professors a ridiculous amount of money to put up with your heathen children," Philip smarted back.

"Well in that case, I would like that very much," Martha said in a more serious tone.

"Around five then?"

"Five it is.'

Philip watched from his front door as she made her way around the corner and disappeared from sight. She lived almost directly behind him and he couldn't believe he had never taken the time to get to know her before that night.

As he got ready for bed he thought of Martha and what she had said. Then, he began to appreciate exactly how much he had been paying attention to her. He had actually noticed her. He noticed her breast, her hair, and her eyes without even a moment of guilt. A broad smile made its way across his face as he lay back on his bed. Deep in his heart, he knew Elly would approve.

SATURDAY

Philip got out of his warm bed and put on the trench coat his father had left him so many years before. It was always hanging with care on the large brass bedpost at the foot of his bed and was found quite easily in the dark. As he slipped it on, the silk lining tingled the skin of his naked body. Walking from the bedroom and through the dark hall to the front door, he glanced over his shoulder. There, gliding along the wall he saw a shadow. Knowing that the shadow would follow, he turned his collar up and walked out into the cold night air.

As he walked across the porch and down the small walkway, the shadow creature close at hand, a fog as thick as any he had ever known encircled him. The sensation of walking on a cloud filled his mind with grey misty thoughts. For no reason, he turned left on Main. The well paved road seemed different under his bare feet, almost as if it had been dug up and redone with cobblestones.

"This way Mr. Parker," came a voice in the distant mist. "Come this way." It was a soft voice, yet it seemed to pierce the fog with ease.

Philip looked around in confusion. "Forward, Mr. Parker," came the faceless voice, only this time it was more demanding. It was definitely a man's voice, but whose?

Philip became overwhelmed with dread and goose bumps the size of marbles broke out on his arms. What the hell was he doing out here, where did he ever get such a stupid notion.

"Who are you?" Philip yelled into the darkness.

"You shall know me soon enough, NOW COME."

Philip wanted to run back to the safety of his own house, the comfort of his bed, but the voice drew him. He did not want to follow, but the voice had power, overwhelming power that took his will. He continued to follow.

After some distance, how long or how far was hard to judge for he had lost all sense of time and space in the gloomy mist. Philip found himself standing in a field of newly greened clover. The Baker's back forty, thought Philip. That must be where I am. But had he really walked this far so fast? It was impossible for him to tell.

Philip looked around for the shadow creature. He could not see it but he knew it was still there. Strangely, he felt better knowing that, as if the creature was there to protect him from something evil.

From the far side of the field came a light, vague at first, then it grew, illuminating the fog with a slight orange glow. Philip heard a rustling sound close by, he started to turn and see what it was. A small animal, the shadow creature, or maybe someone else had happened upon the sight. As he turned to see, however, the light broke through the fog and into the clearing. Philip wisely hurried back into the safety of the mist.

A cloaked figure, holding a torch, came into Philip's view. It walked slowly, face hidden by a dark hood that covered much of his face. Behind him came another in the same fashion, then another, and another. The procession counted out to twelve. The leader, a large man made his way to the center of the field and there dropped the lit torch into a pile of kindling. At once the field was filled with light and Philip once again moved back deeper into the fog, this time into a small patch of trees where he lay flat upon his belly. At that same moment, he heard another rustling sound. Someone else, or something else, was moving back from the light as well. Philip strained his eyes but could see nothing.

The field became brighter and brighter as flames engulfed the wood, reaching ever higher into the night sky. The twelve hooded figures made a complete circle around the fire and holding one another's hands began swaying back and forth. Suddenly, without warning, there came an ear-shattering scream. From the fog appeared yet another cloaked figure, and with him, bound around the wrist, were two young children. The first was a boy and the second was a girl, both appeared to be around fourteen years old. They were being ruthlessly dragged along by a rope. Though they fought with all their might, the hooded figure had little trouble forcing them along. Once in the full light of the fire, the rest began chanting in some long forgotten language that Philip thought was Latin at first, but realized that was not quite it. It seemed almost animal in nature, like the chant of speaking wolves.

Philips heart began pounding in his chest. He could actually hear it beating, boom boom, boom boom. Sweat began dripping from his forehead, every nerve in his body was alive. Now he knew what it was like to be the hunted rabbit, cowering from the sound of the baying hounds. He knew, if caught, he was a dead man. This had to be it, the cult that killed those two kids in the cemetery.

The children were led to within inches of the fire and there the leader approached them. Slowly he raised his hand and Philip could see hair as white as snow but a youthful face, certainly not older than thirty. Walking over to the screaming children, the man placed his hands on top of their heads and the two became silent at once, almost domicile. They stood there like statues without moving or making a sound. The others in the band removed their hoods as well and raised their hands to the sky. From where he lay, Philip could make out five women and six men, all with the look of youth, even though four had silver hair like the first.

"This is the night we have been waiting for, my family," said the leader. His voice was loud and full, his hands were still on the heads of the children. "Tonight we complete the covenant." He looked at the two below him and grinned a hideous grin. "Master Fritz, come forward."

A figure, that Philip had yet to see in clear view, moved around the fire to where the leader stood. He was young and handsome, with soft blue eyes and long curly blonde hair. He fell to his knees in front of the man, put his head between the man's legs, and hugged him tightly.

"Arise Master Fritz," spoke the leader, "Behold." he said to the rest. "The thirteenth, the covenant will be complete, the Judas has come to us. He shall be my successor, with the power that keeps us out of the hands of those who would end our reign on earth. They tried to destroy us in the streets of Europe, in the hills of Zion, and the temples of Egypt. But they cannot stop us, for our god is the only true power, the only true master."

The rest began to cheer and dance at the words of their leader and in the naked firelight, their shadows darted to and fro across the field.

"We have lost our brother Master Bacon to the flame, but tonight, we have a new brother in Master Fritz." As more shouts rose from the strange group, the leader held Fritz's face in his hands and kissed him hard on the lips. "The time has come for you Master Fritz. The boy first. He reeks of purity like the girl." Then in a softer voice he added, "Before we partake, the good earth must be made unholy."

Philip watched in horror as Fritz gazed upon the young lad with hungry blue eyes. From his robe he pulled a large pointed dagger in the shape of a ram's horn. The motionless boy did not flinch as Fritz rubbed the blade over his cheek. In a quick downward motion, Fritz cut the rags loose from the boy's body, leaving him standing naked in the cool night air. The group cheered. Slowly, Fritz ran his free hand up and down the boy's taut body. The boy slowly started to come out of his trance, his eyes cleared and his body began to tremble. He started to scream, but never got the chance. With one swipe from his blade, Fritz slashed open the boy's throat. The leader grabbed the boy from behind and held him while his blood gushed from his body and fell into a thick red pool. The band cheered even louder. All this time the girl had remained silent, not aware of what was going on next to her. Now Fritz turned his gaze to her.

Philip was fighting an overwhelming urge to scream as the leader finally let the limp body of the boy fall to the ground.

"And now the final rite," spoke the leader.

Fritz cut away the girl's dress.

"That which binds us with him."

Fritz laid the girl on her back in the pool of blood.

"The flesh."

Fritz lowered his face over the girls flat, firm stomach.

"And so a new god is born."

In a flash, Fritz had buried his teeth deep into the girl's stomach and came up with a mouth full of flesh. The band cheered.

"Born in living flesh."

The girl, now awake, looked up into the blood-stained face of Fritz and then down at her own pain and screamed.

"Eternal life is ours."

The rest of the band now fell upon the girl.

Philip could hear her cries ringing in his ears. He tried to cover them but it was no use. Finally, when Philip thought he would lose his mind the noise stopped. Now the deathly quiet made Philip feel more alone than he had ever felt in his life. If only he could have saved them, thought of something. Swiftly there came a different sound, the sound of thundering hooves, the sound of brave riders on bold steeds. They came exploding into the field from all sides. The band scattered but the horsemen ran them down with reckless abandon.

A priest rode to a stop just to the right of Philip, so close he could have reached out and touched the hooves of his pure white steed. Above his head he held a large crucifix, which seemed to generate its own light. It took Philip a moment to place what he was looking at. The horsemen were dressed in red coat attire and the banner they waved was that of King George.

A tall rider came riding up from the attack. "I only count eleven your grace. Two have made it to the woods."

"God help us, we must find them," replied the Priest.

"Yes, Your Grace," said the rider, and the two sped off together across the field.

Philip began to feel nauseated and he moved gradually back into the patch of trees. From behind him, he heard the loud crack of a broken twig. He swung around only to be gazing directly into the eyes of Fritz. The blueness of his eyes matched only by the redness of his chin.

Then Philip did scream. That's what awoke him, the scream.

In the wee hours before dawn, little Scotty Cooper was already hard at work with his morning chores. There was twice the work to do when his brother was away. Thankfully, he was due back today, and he knew his Pa would beat him good if it was not done by the time he got up. Josh Cooper, Scotty's father, was well liked in the community for his kindness, however, that did not include his own family. To look at him, you would never guess that Scotty was the child of classic abuse. Josh Cooper had been careful to keep the marks well hidden and if asked, Scotty and Timmy, his brother of thirteen, would say nothing. Often there is a very thin line between love and hate that can get lost and tossed about in a child's mind. What is normal anyway? Was there not love in their father's fist? At times, Josh Cooper could be as nice as any father. Other times, mostly after drinking, he would get that cold glare in his beady brown eyes. The two boys had learned to stay away from him when Pa was in one of his moods, but they often came without warning. Josh could go from a happy mood to a violent fit of anger in the snap of a finger. Sometimes he would then try to make amends, but his kind words often fell on deaf ears. Sally Cooper had lived with it for ten years before she finally slipped away in the night leaving everything, including her two young sons.

This morning, however, Scotty knew he was safe. Pa had been out drinking half the night with his buddies down at Jones's, spending money that could have gone to a new pair of shoes or pants for him and his brother. There was no way he would be up before noon. In the meantime, Scotty could enjoy his favorite time of day, alone in the old beaten down barn with his favorite animals. There was Tiger and Lemon Drop, the two cats who were kept to keep the mice down and the rats away; Dodger, the family dog; Lightning the horse; and of course, Daisy, the family cow. There were always the chickens to feed and the hogs to slop, but Scotty's favorites always got theirs first.

Daisy was in need of milking. Her utter was full and Scotty barely had to touch her before she released into the pail. When he was done he set the pail down on the stool and walked over to Lightning. First, a quick brushing and then a little straw was in order. As Scotty ran his hand over the horses back, he noticed it was in a cold sweat. Must be coming down with something, thought Scotty. Pa sure will be pissed off if he has to go to Doc Jordon's. The morning air was still cool and the horse had no reason to sweat other than being ill. Then he remembered an old wives tale he had heard from his grandpa: *Comes a tale from days of old / of when a horse will sweat from cold / sour milk from the utter / stinks of rot, as thick as butter / fret and stew and worry much / for it's a sign of the witch's touch.*

Scotty smiled. He had really loved that old man and all the wives tales he told. He would sit and talk for hours about the old days and the tall stories of his youth. Scotty would listen to every word and never doubt a one. Of course, he was just a kid then, no older than five or six. He was all of ten now and he knew better, still he could not fight the urge. He walked over to where he had placed the pail he had just filled from Daisy and looked inside. At once, his nose filled with a terrible smell. The milk had already gone sour. He tried to slosh it around but it had become solid in a matter of minutes. The phrase *stinks of rot, as thick as butter* stuck in his mind. Scotty felt a cold chill run up his spine. "Come on, Scotty," he said out loud. "This is going too far. There is no such thing as witches."

Surely there was a good explanation for all of this. There was no Santa, no dragons, and there were no witches.

. . . of when a horse will sweat from cold

All right, he said to himself, get your shit together. It's just a fairy tale. I have to worry about getting my work done. Pa will beat me more than any old witch anyway.

Just then, there came a scurrying noise from the rafters. Scotty looked up just in time to see the figure of a man plummeting from up above.

Kip was on his way to Parksville when he got the call. Cowan, who had been in the area, was already on the scene. Though the morning had a chill to it, the day had started getting hot and the sun was beating down. Kip did not know what to expect, but his hopes were that this incident had nothing to do with any cult. If this case did show any signs of a cult, he would have to call in the Feds, something he dreaded. He knew it was the only answer, though he hated the idea. The Feds had a way of bringing up old ghosts in a town like Parksville, old ghosts that were better left in the grave. People had their lives ruined with reckless abandon because no effort would be made to protect those who could be hurt by having their past become common knowledge. Kip knew that everyone had their dark places, and he did not think it was fair that others were allowed to exploit them in the name of justice. Still, the case would be too big to handle through the local police department. An isolated murder, even an unusually vicious one, was a local matter. But if there was a trend developing, they had to do whatever it took to put an end to it. Prior to the murders of Bud Kennedy and Samantha Hasting, murder in Parksville had been unheard of; if there was another, it would devastate the community and panic would soon set in.

He arrived at the Cooper farm around noon. Officer Cowan had arrived a short time before and was standing in front of an old, rundown barn with a man Kip knew at once, Josh Cooper. The two had gone to school together and even though he had not lain eyes on the man for a very long time, he remembered his face at once. No one ever forgot the school bully. A hate that Kip thought had passed some time ago returned in all its glory. Maybe the years had changed the man, but in his heart, Kip didn't believe it for a minute.

Kip walked straight past Josh Cooper and Cowan without saying a word. He had only one thing on his mind; he had to see the boy. His fear was acting like a magnet, drawing him into the barn, toward the nightmare he was afraid was awaiting him there.

A sigh of relief escaped Kip as he looked down on little Scotty Cooper's body. He lay on his back in the hay in Lighting's stall. His eyes were open and looking straight up but the body was intact. In fact, there was no apparent cause of death.

Even though the gate was wide open, the horse seemed reluctant to escape. He was backed up to the wall as far as possible from the boy's body.

"Sir, that's how his father found him this morning."

Kip did not bother to turn around, he knew Cowan's gentle voice. Instead, he got down on one knee and looked at the boy's face. He looked like his father when he was younger.

"The MED Unit is on its way and I called Sam." Cowan said.

From the front of the barn there was a loud uproar. Timmy Cooper, who had just returned from camp, was standing at the open door shouting into his father's face. Josh swung his open hand and knocked the older boy to the ground. Young Cooper was not so easily silenced and got up screaming once more.

"You finally did it, you son of a bitch. You killed him."

"You hush your mouth boy, before I let you have it good." Josh then added in a quieter voice, "I had nothing to do with this."

"You liar. You killed my brother. You're a fucking liar." By now, Timmy was in his father's reddened face once more.

Josh raised his hand again, but this time it was caught in the back swing by Kip, Timmy, who had taken a step back to avoid the blow, was wiping the snot from his nose with the back of his hand. Tears were pouring down his face and he attacked his father again with words broken up by his uncontrollable sobbing. "What did he do this time, forget to make your coffee, or maybe he forgot to do the wash. Is that why he got it this time, is that why my brother's dead, answer me you son of a bitch!"

"I told you I didn't touch him." Josh turned to Kip, "The boy's over taken with grief, that's all."

Kip stung him with a doubtful look.

"Oh yeah," shouted Timmy. "Then why don't you try to explain this." Quickly, the boy turned and undid the buttons to his pants. Before Josh or anyone else could stop him they fell into the dirt. Then, with one quick pull the boy's briefs followed. There he stood naked to the world pointing his buttocks at Kip. All the evidence was there, bruises and scars that looked like they belonged to a slave who had undergone the whip. When the boy turned around, Kip could see bruises that reached from the boy's pelvis to his testicles and inner thighs. Without a pause, Timmy sat down on the ground. He pulled off his old shoes and tattered socks revealing feet scarred with any number of unattended cigarette burns.

Rodney Wetzel

"He did this to me," blubbered Timmy, "and if you look at Scotty you'll find more, fresh ones too I'll bet."

Josh Cooper just stood there, he knew he could say nothing in his own defense.

Kip, however, did not have any trouble finding the words he was looking for. He turned to Cowan and said, "Book this piece of shit."

Cowan read him his rights and then coarsely cuffed his hands behind his back.

Unexpectedly, from inside the barn came a loud squawk, Kip turned just in time to see an outsized crow fly through the open door. It headed straight for Josh and landed on the man's head. The crow fearlessly started pecking at his face. Kip and Cowan just stood there for a moment in disbelief, too stunned to move. Josh was powerless to do anything to ward off the attack because his hands were cuffed tightly behind him. He was turning around wildly and shaking his head back and forth trying to shake the bird loose. Cowan recovered her wits and took her night stick to the beast. Then the bird just flew away, having done some amount of mutilation to Josh's face. Kip watched the bird until it was out of sight. By that time, Cowan had the bleeding Cooper in the back of her squad car.

"Have you ever?" asked Cowan. "We'll have to go to the hospital. I think that bird was trying to dig his eyes out."

Kip stood there and didn't say a word.

Sam Helman, the city Coroner and the ambulance pulled in. They parked both vehicles behind Kip's car.

"Thank God," said Cowan "I have no idea how to write this one up.

Philip arrived at the Lake's house at five, on the nose. He had considered forgetting the whole affair. After what had taken place the night before, he was not quite sure he wanted to spend time with anyone. The dream this morning had not faded when he woke up. He remembered it, all of it, every morbid detail. It was so clear in his mind, he could have recited every word, described every action. But most of all, he could not get those eyes out of his mind.

Philip tried to shake it off as he got out of his car. He was dressed in his favorite jeans and sports shirt. Walking up to the door he made his final check to make sure everything was in order. He straightened his belt and ran his hand through his hair. Knocking on the front door, he was sure that Martha had changed her mind. I'm sorry Philip, but I have a headache, then he would go home to drown himself in a six-pack, forget this whole day had ever happened. Just then, Franky opened the door.

"Hi," he said with a smile so broad that Philip was almost embarrassed. "Mom is upstairs getting ready."

Franky, showed the nervous Philip into the living room where he sat on the oversized recovered sofa. Philip thought he could feel a broken spring somewhere beneath him.

"Can I get you a coke or a beer?" asked Franky, still grinning ear to ear. He obviously thought the idea of his mother dating his professor was a little funny.

"No, thank you." Philip answered politely.

Franky walked into the hall, and from where he sat, Philip could hear him yelling up the stairway: "He's here."

Franky returned to the living room and sat directly across from Philip all the time rubbing his hands together trying not to stare.

"So, you and mom are going out to dinner?"

"Yeah, I guess we are."

"Where are you taking her," Franky was obviously trying to make conversation to relax Philip but came off sounding like a father sending his daughter on her first date with the town juvenile delinquent.

"I don't know, wherever she wants to go, I guess."

"She likes Italian, why don't you try Emeils?"

"Sounds all right to me." Philip knew he sounded as uncomfortable as he felt. He had this kid in his class three times a week, but now sitting in the same room with him was making his crazy. Maybe it was the way he kept saying Mom.

"Hi Philip," came Martha's voice from the hall, "sorry to keep you waiting." She was dressed in a modest cotton dress laced with thin silk. The shade matched her shoes and purse. She had not gone all out, but she had spent some time in making herself look good.

"Is this all right?" she asked as she turned around. "I didn't know where we were going so I wore this, I can go almost anywhere in this."

"It's fine." Philip said. He was very impressed, and it showed.

"Good," she replied. "Shall we go, then? I am starving to death, did you bring your professor's credit card?" she added with a smile.

They both snickered, and Franky just shook his head at the two and went upstairs.

Kip arrived at Sam Helman's house around eight. He was flabbergasted the man had offered to meet him there instead of at the morgue where Sam worked, but was more than happy at the invitation. Kip had always felt sorry for the man. At the age of twenty-two, Sam was involved in a car accident, leaving him scarred for life. The car he was driving had skidded off the road and flipped a number of times and burst into flames. It had left over two thirds of the man's face covered with scar tissue making him like someone out of a horror movie. For this reason, Sam had kept pretty much to himself and had never married. But he had his own house and took great pains to maintain a family atmosphere. It had a very homey feel to it.

Sam wasted no time. He led Kip into the kitchen, poured them both a cup of coffee and went straight to work.

"I got the test back on those two kids," said Sam, taking a seat across the table. "The boy died from the wound on his neck. He bled to death plain and simple."

"No bruises, or signs of a struggle?"

"Just the hole the stake made in his feet," Sam stated. "You were right about the girl though, she did appear to be eaten. The only problem is, we can't prove it."

"What exactly do you mean by that?"

"No saliva." Sam shifted slightly in his chair and then leaned forward. "You see, I checked the radius of the alleged bites, it could be human, but without saliva there is no way to say it was, and no way to say it wasn't for that matter. We don't know of anything human or animal that wouldn't leave at least a trace of saliva. But if that was a human, it had the sharpest damn teeth I've ever seen. It looks like she was torn to shreds with a razor blade."

"Any sign of a struggle there?"

"None."

"No skin under the finger nails, nothing?"

"Nothing, either she was unaware of what was taking place or realized it too late."

"How could anyone be unaware of that, I mean look at her. Even if she had let someone do that to her willingly, which is hard to imagine, how could she not be aware enough to struggle against the pain."

"Well, it looks like it was over quickly, but to tell you the truth, I don't know. I do know that there were no drugs to calm her. Both she and the boy where clean."

"What about the other kid we got today, have you had a chance to look at him yet?"

"Sure, I looked at him." A look of sadness crossed his face and he looked away for just a moment. "I shouldn't say this without a full autopsy, but have you ever heard that story about the little boy who just gave up one day and died?"

"You mean like that movie they always showed in Psych class?"

"Yeah, you know that one. Well, I think maybe that's what happened here. Look, I know I sound crazy, but I looked that boy up one side and down the other. His father had beat him, the signs were all there, but it was nothing that should have killed him. Maybe when I cut him open I will find something, but I gotta tell you, I just don't think I will. His father still wants the autopsy I take it?"

"Well, he still says he had nothing to do with it and wants to prove it. Maybe your theory is right."

"Maybe, but there's something else . . ."

"What?"

"Nothing, just some difficulties I'm having."

Kip looked at Sam. Sam's eyes seemed to mist over. Maybe it was because Sam was lost for an explanation, maybe it was because he could relate to how the boy felt, or maybe it was the fact that Sam would have given anything to have a family and to see one wasted, was more than he could stand. Still, whatever it was soon passed and Sam smiled at Kip.

"By the way, what happened to that Cooper guy, anyway? When the med team took him away his face was a bloody mess."

Kip took a deep breath and began to tell him the extraordinary story about the bird.

SUNDAY

Franky heard his mother as she came in. He rolled over and looking at the clock on his night stand, saw that it was 6:00 a.m. He thought about going downstairs and razzing her about staying out all night but then thought better of it. It was nice to see her having a good time for a change. It had been some time since he had seen that look of excitement and anticipation on his mother's face. The night before, she was totally alive, waiting for Professor Parker to get there. Franky could tell she really liked him, and that was more than all right with him. He knew Professor Parker was a man that he could really look up to and admire. Besides, if he went down now she would know that he knew she was out all night and he didn't want to embarrass her. He just lay back quietly on his bed. He did not have to be up for another hour anyway. Maybe they will end up getting married, he thought and was surprised that he was very comfortable with the thought.

Franky was meeting Sue at the truck stop at eight. She had called last night saying she had decided to take him up on his offer to help her find an apartment and of course, Franky was more than willing to devote his Sunday helping her. Deep down, he knew that Sue could never fall for a guy like him, but he still felt good just being close to her. And besides, miracles do happen.

Listening to his mother downstairs as she walked around the kitchen, Franky could have sworn he heard her tenderly singing. He ended up getting out of bed fifteen minutes early because he could not take the suspense any more. He made enough clatter getting dressed to make sure his mother knew he was up and around. He figured that way, if she wanted to go to her room and close the door, she could do it before he got downstairs and not give herself away. When he got downstairs, however, there she sat at the kitchen table still dressed in the same outfit she had worn the night before. She did not pay any attention when he walked in. She only sat there with a faraway look in her eyes.

"Ma," Franky teased, "were you out all night?'

Martha continued to look at that spot located in her own mind and responded, "Yes, and it was wonderful."

"Mother!"

"That Philip is one sweet guy. We sat up and watched *The Late Show* and then *The Late Late Show* and then . . ."

"Never mind, Mom, I get the picture."

"He didn't even try to get in my pants." Then she added with a grin, "But, there's always next time."

"Mom, I'm not sure this is a conversation you should be having with your son."

"Oh, come on. You're a big boy now, Franky. You don't have to act so shocked. After all, I'm not dead you know."

"I know, but . . ."

"You know," she interrupted, "you could learn a lesson from Philip."

"What's that?" He asked, although at this point he wasn't entirely sure he wanted the answer.

"You don't have to sleep with a girl to make her feel desirable."

With that, she got up, kissed him lightly on the forehead and headed to the bathroom.

Now he knew he was right earlier, she was singing again. With a big smile on his face, he turned and walked out the door.

Franky arrived early to the truck stop, he knew he would but he was not going to risk being late, either. He sat at the counter running the length of the restaurant's front. In front of him was the waitress station complete with cups, glasses, silverware, the fountain machine, milk machine, coffee maker, trays, salt shakers, pepper shakers, sugar containers, napkins, items for to-go orders and any number of other items, each one carefully placed. He watch as the waitress worked, each knowing the exact location of every item, sometimes not even looking at what they were reaching for. It seemed like a dance that only they knew the steps to. Behind him, he saw large windows along each side. On the small strips of wood in between each window, there were hung prints of Indians, horses, and cowboys. Franky counted a total of nine tables in back and one large round one, just behind him.

He sat and watched the people coming and going out the front door. There were truck drivers, locals that Franky had seen many times around town, business men in suites and families on vacation. It was amazing to him the multicolored tapestry of people walking through these doors every day.

Across the parking lot was the service station with gas in the front for cars and diesel in the back for trucks. The back had five Islands with ten pumps, and they all seemed to be full while he was there. Outside he saw the pump jockeys thumping tires, pumping fuel, checking oil and washing windshields. Rough job, thought Franky, man it must be a bitch in the winter.

Unlike Franky, Sue was not punctual, arriving almost twenty minutes late. Franky did not seem to care if she was late, he was just glad she was there at all. It made his whole day to see her appealing face come gliding through the door.

"Hi Franky," she said walking up to the table, "I'm sorry I'm late, but I just couldn't get myself stirring this morning."

"That's okay. I didn't get here myself until just a minute ago." The big gorilla of a waitress that was just pouring his fifth cup of coffee shot him a look that told him she had his number. Franky paid no attention to her because he had all of his attention firmly fixed on Sue.

"Well good. Listen, I hate to rush you, but are you ready to get going?"

"Sure, why not," said Franky. He got up and threw two dollars on the table to pacify the necromancer and headed for the door right behind Sue.

"Wow," Franky said, looking down on Sue's Porsche, "I thought you had a Firebird?"

"I do," she said "but I had to take it in this morning, this is just a loner, I don't care for them myself."

"Oh, I do."

Sue threw the keys to Franky and said, "Here, you drive then. I never drive myself when I have a gentleman around to do it for me."

"Are you sure?" asked Franky.

"Sure, I'm sure." With that, she climbed in the passenger's side.

Franky liked the way this day was turning out. He got in and started it up. Franky had always been a good driver, but the muscle this thing had would take a little getting used to.

While Franky and Sue where pulling out of the truck stop, Jimmy Martinez was just finishing giving head to a sixty-five-year-old trucker in the men's bathroom. He really did not like doing this, but ten bucks was ten bucks, at least this one didn't want to stick it up his ass. That hurt like a bitch. He wouldn't have to do this shit if his momma would just give him some money once in a while, but no, she said he would only get in trouble if she gave him money. What a bitch.

The trucker, zipping up his pants, put a ten spot on the back of the toilet then turned and walked out. "I'll be back in a week," he heard him say as he passed through the door.

Jimmy got up and walked over to the sink and tried to wash the taste out of his mouth. He wandered how much those damn lot lizards were making a night. He saw them two or three times a week, three girls from Jackson that walked around, knocking on truck doors, asking for a good time. I bet they got a lot for a blowjob. He heard one say she got a twenty just for a hand job.

After trying to flush his mouth, Jimmy took out one of his non-filtered camels and lit it. He knew there was no smoking in the bathroom, but he didn't care. One of these days, he was going to stick that old man and take all his money. He could too; he had a Bowie at home that could carve him up like an Easter ham. Sick old bastard deserved it.

Without warning, the feeling he had down by the lake came rushing through his body, something was not right. Over the already strong odor of the dirty men's room came that smell, the smell of rotting flesh and the feeling of being watched, the feeling of being hunted. Just then, Jimmy noticed in the small tinted window above his head, a large black bird staring down at him.

There were only three apartments Franky knew were for rent in Parksville. One was over the Barber Shop, one was down in the new subdivision next to his Aunt Joyce's old house and the other, of course, was the one at old lady Cartwright's, which just happened to be directly across the street from his house. He would take her there first.

Old lady Cartwright came to the front door dressed in a robe and fuzzy slippers. Her gray hair was pulled back in a comb and her eyes still had not cleared the sleep from them.

"Well, Franky. What brings you here?" she asked as she opened the door completely exposing her large frame more fully.

Franky gave her a broad smile. He and the saucy old woman had been the best of friends since he was just a little boy. He had made many trips across the street for a visit, and maybe a cookie or piece of cake while he was there.

"This is a friend of mine from school." Franky explained. As he introduced the two, the old toothless woman held out her hand and Sue shook it.

"You can just call me Brandy dear, although I understand that most of the young people around here refer to me as Old Lady Cartwright. Never to my face, of course."

Franky shifted his position a little and tried to look as if that was news he was hearing for the first time.

"Sue is interested in the apartment," he finally explained.

"How nice. Won't you both come in?"

Once inside the door, Brandy took Franky aside. "Is this your girlfriend, Franky?" She asked just above a whisper. Then she added insult to injury by reaching up and pinching his already flushed cheek.

Brandy had spent most of her life in New Orleans, working in the red light district. She had started her career as a dancer but ended up running the largest brothel in the city. At the ripe old age of fifty-five, Brandy had retired and moved back to the place of her birth. Though the town's people never really knew how she had spent her years away, not that she gave a shit what they thought, she had insulated herself from the town and avoided most people like the plague. There were some she tolerated and even a few she liked, like Martha and the nice man she had married, but for the most part, she had no use for them. It was not the fact that she might be shunned, she didn't care about that; it was just the fact that she was ready for some peace and quiet. That self-induced solitude did not include the local children; however, she adored them. She had never had the time, or the life style to have children when she was younger and never regretted it. But still, she liked the way they were full of life and innocence. From time to time, they reminded her of how good life could be. She had watched Franky grow up and of all the neighborhood children, Franky was her favorite.

"No," Franky whispered back, "just a friend."

"Shame, she sure is a looker," teased Brandy.

Brandy led the two up the stairs to the apartment and as she unlocked the door to let them in, Franky could not hold back his astonishment at what he saw. He had not been in the apartment for a long time, not since his cousin Bobby Martin had lived there. Back then it was more like a cheap motel room than an apartment, but now it was a sight to behold. She had redone the apartment in all white with black leather furniture and even a black lacier wet bar. The carpet must have been a foot thick and the walls even exhibited some original prints.

"I've done some work to it since you were here last, Franky." As she walked them through, Franky was amazed at the changes. The kitchen had a wicker table with a glass top and chairs and came complete with a dishwasher and microwave. The bedroom held a king-size waterbed with a canopy and the old, back porch had been converted into a large deck overlooking the back yard.

"It's beautiful," said Sue.

"Thank you, dear," answered Brandy.

"You wouldn't know from the outside that this house is so big and . . ."

"Pleasant. I know it is a fright on the outside but the bastards raise my taxes every damn time I even put a coat of paint on it. By the way, if you take the apartment, the receipts may be a little off, if you know what I mean. But don't worry, I always write paid in full on it."

Franky was a blissful man. He could tell just by looking at Sue that she really adored the apartment.

"I gotta tell you right up front that it doesn't come cheap," said Brandy. "I have spent a lot of dough fixing this place up."

"How much?" Sue asked.

"Three hundred fifty, and you pay your own utilities."

Franky felt his heart drop. There must be a dozen one-bedroom apartments around for a lot less money. There went all his dreams of having a perfect summer.

"I'll take it." came Sue's reply.

Sam looked down at the body of Scotty Cooper. He had tried to tell Kip what was going on, but pushed it off as "some difficulties." Some difficulties, he laughed. There was no explanation for what he saw. Even though the boy had been dead for more than twenty-four hours, there were no signs of rigor mortis, discoloration or decay. There was no doubt the boy was deceased, there were no vital signs. Still Sam could not bring himself to do the autopsy. He had started more than once, but he stopped every time. There was something deep inside him that would not let him start cutting the adolescent up. Although they needed to find a cause of death and currently had the unexplained mystery of how the body was preserving itself after death, there was no way he could put that knife into the boy without feeling like he was committing murder. There was something unnatural about him, living or dead. Sam had sat and stared at the lifeless body all day, looking for an explanation, but he still did not have any solutions. He quietly turned off the overhead light, walked to his desk and sat down. And then for no reason, he put his head in his hands and began to cry.

While Franky and Sue were looking at the apartment, a block away, Philip lay awake on his bed. He had just woken up and was still hesitant to move. The sun was shining in his window and the air was full of singing birds. Softly, his thoughts turned to Martha and what a magnificent woman she was. If he was not cautious, he would fall head-over-heels in love with this lady. He had thought about asking her to spend the night, and he was thinking about more than watching movies. But he was afraid. Not of a performance problem, the bulge in his pants he fought hard to conceal more than once during the evening had been proof of that. What he was afraid of was taking a chance on falling asleep afterwards. He would feel like a complete ass if he woke up screaming at the top of his lungs. The dream from the night before had still not passed, and Philip doubted the dreams had stopped. Until he was sure they had, he would avoid sleeping in the same house with her. He was more than ready and felt that she would be willing too, although she seemed glad that nothing had happened that first night. It made him smile to think that right now, she was probably thinking he was a perfect gentleman instead of a coward with lurid thoughts, afraid to be taken for a nut if he acted on them.

Philip felt refreshed after a couple of hours of dreamless sleep. For the first time in four nights, he had gotten some greatly needed rest, even if it had been a short night. One thought kept bothering him: why no dreams last night? Maybe they had stopped. A cold chill crept along his spine telling him that he was way off base. The dream and the murder of those two kids were connected. He did not know how he knew this, but he suddenly knew that he was as sure as he knew his own name. This is irrational, he thought, maybe dreams were an insight into your own psych, but they sure as hell could not tell you about a murder case. He tried to rationalize that the dreams were caused by seeing those photographs in Kip's office then remembered that the dreams had started before he saw those pictures. He tried to dismiss the whole idea of there being a connection between the dreams and the murders but was not able to convince himself. "You are being a fool." He said aloud. "A dream is just a dream." Still, those eyes, those haunting blue eyes. The phone rang and Philip almost shot out of his skin.

He pulled up to Briskey Lake at eleven-thirty. It had been a very distraught Kip who had made the call that had scared him out of his wits. "There's something here you have to see." Is all Kip would say and no doubt something big was going on. As he came over the last hill before the lake, he saw a large number of police cars parked across the large open field next to the lake. Men were walking this way and that searching the ground and policing the area for the smallest bit of evidence. The area around the Yorkey's cottage had been marked off with bright yellow tape and only two figures stood inside the colorful barricade. Philip recognized one of the figures as Kip and pulled his MG up next to his rusted-out Pontiac. As he started over to the restricted area, he was stopped at once by Officer Cowan.

"I'm sorry sir, but you can't . . ."

"It's all right," said Kip coming up behind her. "This is our expert in the occult I told you about."

Philip smiled. He was no more an expert on the occult than he was an expert on physics. He just happened to teach a couple of classes in world religions, but obviously Kip felt he needed his help and Philip was not going to let him down.

Cowan smiled a welcome and went back to what she was doing before Philip arrived. Kip walked over to Philip and put his arm around him to lead him to the front of the cottage.

"I'm sorry to bother you with this but, if you can help us in anyway, it would be greatly appreciated."

The two came to a stop right in front of the Yorkey's front steps.

There laying on the ground, covered with a white blanket was a large body.

There was only one person Philip knew who had a frame that large so it came as no shock when Kip pulled back the sheet and revealed the half eaten body of Bill Smith. The left side of his skull was crushed inwards as if caught in a large vise and then squeezed. Below, tiny fragments of bone stuck out where his rib cage had once been.

Philip ran to the lake and vomited. After the nausea subsided a little, he raised his head and glanced over the lake. His eyes focused on the old manor until he trusted himself to be able to talk.

"My God, what the hell is going on here?" He said at last as he made his way back from the lake. "This is just down the road from that damn cemetery."

"I was hoping you could tell us," Kip replied.

Philip turned his eyes and looked into the unsympathetic water of Briskey Lake and for one fleeting moment, he thought he saw the lake looking back at him, holding him in a trance with a pair of crisp blue eyes. Quickly, he turned his head and when he looked back, he saw nothing but water. Philip let out a deep breath.

"What's the matter?" asked Kip.

"Oh . . . nothing, it's just that man is my neighbor."

"We know, we just found his wallet in his pants. You don't know what he was doing here do you?"

"No, no I don't." Answered Philip. Poor Sally, even if she did recover from her attempted suicide, this news was going to kill her.

"Well, whoever is doing this, must be a couple of strong mothers. It would take a lot to bring that guy down. We found him at the water's edge, even Sam will have a bitch of time trying to figure out if the guy drowned first or . . ."

"Look," said Philip, "I still think the answer lies somewhere in that old cemetery."

Kip started to say something but changed his mind.

"That place still scares you doesn't it? You remember that day we went there as kids don't you?"

"Yes, I remember," Kip said avoiding Philip's eyes.

"What was it? What scared you so bad that day? You never did tell me what happened."

"Oh, come on Philip, that was years ago."

"Look, I know it sounds stupid to bring it up after all this time and at this particular moment, but you were scared, more scared than I have ever seen anyone in my life. Now I want to know why."

Kip started to answer, but just then, Cowan came shouting on a dead run. "We found two more in the house across the lake."

The walk around the lake was silent. Philip did not mention the cemetery again, and Kip did not offer to finish what he started to say. Though Cowan had offered to drive the two men, they had decided to walk it instead. The walk would give them time to think, time to remember, but more importantly, time to prepare themselves for what they knew they were going to see when they got there. The Gibsons had been dear old friends to them both, and now they were certainly torn apart. When they reached the spot in the road where it forked, one road leading around the lake and the other toward the old cemetery, both men looked almost involuntarily toward the cemetery, but not a word was said. As they reached the Richardson's house, Philip had a disturbing thought: what if they had returned early from Virginia?

He ran up their drive and started looking in windows. Kip knew immediately what Philip was thinking. He knew his men had already checked the area, but he too felt the need to check for himself. The house was pleasant and neat and the furniture was still covered in white sheets, just the way the Richardsons had left it. If they had returned home the first thing they would have done was uncover the furniture. Besides, there was no blue Ford in the garage. Both men felt comforted that they had not returned yet.

As they finally reached the last twenty yards before the Gibson's house, the silence was finally broken by Kip. "I can still hear old man Gibson screaming at us to stay out of his garden."

"Yeah, but that was nothing compared to getting in his strawberry patch. Remember that day he tanned our asses for that?" Philip asked.

Both men began to laugh at the memory, then stopped when they realized where they were going and why.

"I'm going to call in the Feds, Phil," said Kip. "I have no choice now. I'll try not to involve you if at all possible."

"Don't worry Kip. Everything is going to turn out all right. They are going to find these creeps."

"Do you still think it could be a cult?" Kip inquired.

"More than ever. Like you said, no one person could bring down Bill Smith."

Officer Cowan was standing at the front door. Her face was void of any color as she leaned against the railing of the front steps for support. She had obviously taken it upon herself to have a look before they arrived.

"How bad, Cowan?" asked Kip.

"Sir, you're not going to believe it."

As the two men marched up the steps to the front door, Kip turned to Philip, "You don't have to do this Philip."

"Yeah Kip, I think I do."

The first thing to hit them as they entered the small, modest home was the stench. It was thick and stung their noses with a sharp sickening odor.

"They must have been dead a few days." said Philip.

"No, they were fine the day the two kids were killed, I talked to them myself." Kip quickly replied. "Where are they?" he now asked of Cowan.

Cowan pointed to the back bedroom but made no move to go with them.

As they walked down the small hallway toward the rear of the house the stench became overwhelming. Flies, just awakening from their winter sleep, filled the air with an unsettling sound. Even before they reached the door, the carpet under their feet was stained red with blood, which had oozed out from under it. Slowly, Kip opened the door. The room was covered with blood, the walls, the floor, even the ceiling. On the bed, they saw the Gibsons. Both were in fact partially eaten, the same as the others, but this time, like a sick joke, the heads had been ripped off their bodies and were placed in a lewd fashion between their legs. Their old, wrinkled bodies were propped up by pillows and their hands placed on their heads as if they were performing an unnatural sex act upon themselves.

Both men stood in total shock for a full minute and then Kip slammed the door shut hard enough to rattle the whole house. "Where in the hell is Sam?" He shouted at Cowan.

"I've been trying to reach him but . . ."

"You find him and you get his ass down here now. I want this cleaned up as fast as possible."

"But sir, if the Feds are going to be called in they are going to want to see this."

"Move your ass, Cowan."

"Yes sir." She thought about saying something else but one look at her boss was enough to convince her to change her mind.

"I don't care if they do get pissed, no one else is going to see them like this." He said to himself. "Maybe I'll just have to wait a while before I make that call."

As Kip turned around, there on the floor sat Philip curled into a fetal position. Kip sat down next to him and put his arm around his shoulders. "We are going to find the bastards that did this just wait and see. And when we do, God have mercy, because I sure as hell won't."

"They're starting to enjoy it."

"What?" asked Kip confused.

"Look at those two kids, no sign of a struggle. Then Bill, look what they did to him. For some reason they wanted him to fight. Now look at the Gibsons. This time they seemed to make a game out of it." Philip got to his feet with new determination and looking down at Kip he added, "It's getting too easy for them."

Kip stood up too. "What do you think they will try next?"

"I have no idea, but there is no question that they will kill again."

"Well, we'll have to put the curfew in effect and pray that the Feds can find them before they do it again."

Philip looked at Kip with an inquisitive expression. "I still think there is something in the cemetery that we have overlooked. I don't know why, but I'm sure the answer is there, somewhere."

Kip had seen the determination in Philip's face. "So what are we waiting for?"

As the two men got ready to leave, Philip thought he heard a voice deep in his mind. *That which binds* *us with him, the flesh.* Philip tried to shake it off. *And so a new God is born.* The dream, it was from the dream.

Philip felt a gust of cold air as he entered the iron gates of Parksville Cemetery. "They look so real don't they?" he said, looking up at the stone lions.

"Yeah, sure, I guess so," answered Kip.

"You know, I never noticed it before, but look at how they were placed."

"I don't get you, what do you mean?"

"They're backwards. You always see stone lions facing outward, but these are facing into the cemetery.

"I still don't get it."

"Lions are a symbol of protection, to ward off danger or evil. These look like they were put here to keep something in instead of keeping something out."

"That or the poor slob who put them in was drunk."

"Yeah, maybe you're right. I'm starting to get carried away with all this."

The spring grass had all but hidden the rubble of stone that was the old section of the cemetery. The old oak tree where the body of Bud Kennedy had been impaled was stained red with his blood. The place seemed somehow ominous to Kip, who stood with his face white as death, lost in his own uneasy thoughts.

"Maybe now you can tell me what happened that day," Philip quietly suggested.

"I knew you were going to bring that up," said Kip looking down at the ground. "I remember, God do I remember."

For the next ten minutes Kip retold the terror of that day when they had played there as kids, the evil power he felt and the cries for freedom he had heard. He also told him of how he felt an overwhelming urge to surrender his will to this malignant power.

"Do you feel it now? Is it still here?"

"Don't be ridiculous. I was just a kid then, having a kid's nightmare. I scared myself."

"Okay, so it was a childhood scare. Now tell me, do you feel it now?"

Kip thought about it for a minute then answered, "No."

"What about the day you found the kids?"

"No, not then either."

Philip hung his head. "I'm sorry, I'm letting myself get carried away again. It's just this damn cemetery. I know the answer is here somewhere, I just feel it in my guts."

"Well, we'll never find it standing around talking about the good old days." said Kip as he started searching the area. Philip smiled at his old friend and joined the search.

They looked among the graves, along the iron fencing, and even searched the old caretaker's shed. Nothing. Whatever they had hoped to find was not there to be found. The longer they looked, the more hope they lost and the more beaten they became. Kip knew all along their chances had been slim. If his team could not find a clue, how would they. Soon, they knew the quest would come to an end, and they would go home none the wiser.

"Look," said Kip at last, "I've got some more pictures downtown, maybe that will . . ."

Kip, who had been following close on the heels of Philip as he circled behind the old oak, fell face first onto the new grass. Philip looked and there it was. He rushed past Kip, not offering to help him and fell down on his knees. Pawing at the ground.

"What in the hell are you doing?" asked an astonished Kip, planting his butt on the ground and dusting himself off.

"This is it, this is what you tripped over," Philip said with a strange mixture of glee and dread. In his hand he held a large clod of sod. "It's loose, look, you can pick it up right off the dirt."

"Excuse me, Einstein, but I can't see how this is the answer to the crime. Besides, my elbow hurts."

"Sorry about the elbow, but feel sorry for yourself later, this is important. Someone has been digging here," he said, showing his excitement.

Reality was dawning on Kip, and he asked, "Who would be digging out here?"

"I don't know but, maybe this is the break we've been waiting for. Whoever it was went to a lot of trouble to make sure we didn't notice. How many people would go to the trouble of digging out here and then re-sod the area, and look at it, it's a perfect job, every piece placed right where it belongs. Not even a trace of dirt. Someone is trying to hide something."

Kip, now very interested, crawled over to where Philip sat with a clump of grass in both hands. "I wonder how long ago this was done."

"Not long by the looks of things. See this, the edges have just now started to turn brown, if you hadn't fallen over it we never would have found it."

"Damn, we went over this place that day we found the kids. How in the hell did we miss this? Any chance this was done after those kids were found?"

"It's just a guess, but I don't think so. But don't be so hard on yourself. If we didn't see it today after the edges started to die and turn brown, how could you expect to see it when it was fresh? It was just luck that you were so ungraceful today."

Kip took a step back. It was true, glancing at it now he could see the outline of a grave. Just a moment before, he had stepped blindly over it without a thought. There was just enough room between the tree and the fence, and if Kip had not been circling the tree, the grave would have gone entirely unnoticed. "Well there is only one thing to do," said Kip with more bravado by far than he felt, "we'll have to dig it up."

"I've got a shovel and . . ."

"Now just hold on, there are rules and regulations here. First, we have to find out who's buried here."

"How in the hell do you think you're going to do that? Don't forget, I did a lot of research on Parksville and even this place. Most of the graves in this section are over a hundred and fifty years old. Do you think their families are still around to give permission to dig the damn thing up?"

Kip looked at Philip and nodded, "Okay, you win. But we do this my way. In a few hours, this place will be crawling with FBI. As soon as I leave here, I'm making that call. So, if we're going to do this it has to be tonight. Meet me back here at five. I'll clear out the mess down there," he said, pointing toward the lake. "If those assholes couldn't find this they sure as hell won't find anything down there."

Mrs. Cartwright turned off the television. She could not believe what she had just heard on the noon news: more murders in Parksville. She had moved to the town to get away from this kind of thing and now it was happening here, of all places. They said there was a curfew and that extra cop cars would be stationed throughout the town, they said they'd even brought in the FBI. Who would have ever guessed?

In New Orleans, she had seen more than most and had lived very close to the edge. It was not the kind of thing that she would recommend to anyone, still she was not ashamed of what she did or how she had lived her life. But now, to have this kind of thing going on in Parksville, she shuttered at the thought.

The police will not release any information about the killings. That is what the news had said, but Mrs. Cartwright new that something wicked was going on. Voodoo and witchcraft were still alive and well in her old neighborhood of New Orleans, so why not here. This had all the signs of something unnatural. Somewhere there was someone with a loose screw who heard voices, worshiped the devil, or even thought himself God, and no one would be safe until the bastard was put away.

Just as she thought this there came a noise from upstairs. It sounded like the wings of a bird. At once, she got up to investigate. Grabbing the poker to the fireplace, she sluggishly made her way upstairs. Before she even turned to face the door to the apartment she spotted a large, black bird sitting on the top stairs railing, gawking at her. It had taken her by surprise, and she let out a loud yell. At once the bird was air born and dove toward her. As it did so, Mrs. Cartwright swung at it with the poker just missing it by inches. It circled once more and this time instead of going towards her, it flew upward and straight through the open window at the top of the stairs.

Though not a practicing Christian, she was far from being an atheist. Her fear of both God and Satan where firmly placed; truth be told, she was rather superstitious. In her many years on Earth, she had seen too many things that could not be explained, at least not to her satisfaction. A black bird in the house meant someone was going to die. Someone in this very house.

That killer will come here next, she thought. Deep down, she felt strongly that serial killers were all possessed by demons. How else could someone, for no other reason than their own satisfaction, kill another human unless they themselves were evil? This she could not understand. The press was always saying they are simply psychopaths, but she felt differently. They were the product of evil and now there was a demon among them. One would come to her home next.

She thought about leaving town for a few days and seeing if the police caught him, but if she left, she would be letting this monster drive her out of her house, and that she would not do. No one, no matter who they were, was going to frighten her away. Just then there came a loud knock at the front door.

"Mrs. Cartwright, we have Sue's stuff here, can we bring it up through the front?" asked Franky.

What about the girl? thought Mrs. Cartwright. She should be warned. But how, who would ever believe this? It was all in her mind anyway. Maybe the bird had accidently come through the same open window it flew out of. But the old saying says it's an omen.

"Mrs. Cartwright, are you there?"

"Yes, I'm here," she answered. Slowly, she calmed down and let reality come back to her troubled mind. "Silly old woman," she said to herself.

By five that evening, Philip was making his way on foot down Railroad Street, carrying a shovel over his shoulder. In passing the Yorkey's cottage he glanced over to where his acquaintance had lain just a short time earlier. Nothing remained now but the bright yellow barrier tape and a solitary figure in the shadow, his friend Kip.

"Well, let's get this over with," Kip said as soon as Philip walked up. "I want to get this done before we get caught. There might be some hot shot Fed hanging around, and we would have a bitch of a time explaining what we were up to."

The two men then progressed up to the old tracks, neither speaking. Both harbored their own thoughts about what they were going to find. The cemetery looked more menacing in the long shadows of evening. Again, Philip felt the blast of cold air when passing through the iron gates, only this time, he could have sworn the piercing eyes of the stone sentinels watched his every move.

"This place still gives me the creeps," Kip said.

"Man, is that the understatement of the year," replied Philip. He knew that Kip was still the same person that was so terrified here all those years ago, and was trying now to put on a brave front. He had not had the experience Kip had had all those years before in this very spot but the recent dreams had hit him the same way. He knew what it was like, now, to be truly frightened, and he found a new sympathy for Kip's feelings.

Slowly, the twosome made their way to the back of the cemetery, to the deeper shadows around the oak. The grave had taken on a foreboding air, felt by both men.

"You know," Said Kip, "I've heard there is an old record book at the library in Jackson filled with the history of Parksville. If I had to, I could go down there and see who's really buried here."

"Forget it, I wrote most of it myself, and I'm telling you there are no records of this part of the cemetery."

"But, if no one knew who was here, why would they dig here?"

"Beats me."

"Maybe they were just grave robbers, trying to find something of value. I've heard that people used to be buried with their most prized possessions."

"Yeah, but how does that tie in with the murders?" He pointed his shovel toward the unmarked grave and started to dig.

"Maybe someone knew what they were looking for, and was looking for the same thing."

"You think those kids dug this up don't you?"

"Could be. Maybe they heard something of value was here and came down to collect, only someone else was here, too. They let the kids do all the work of digging it up and waited for them to rip it off the corpse, then they murdered them."

Philip, tired already, started to sweat and had to stop and lean on the handle of the shovel. "What about Bill and the Gibsons'?"

Kip shrugged his shoulders in defeat, "I don't know."

"It would make more sense," Philip theorized, "if they had happened upon someone else digging here and were killed because they saw something they shouldn't have: like a satanic ritual that involved the exhumation of human remains."

"But then, why leave the bodies here? Surely, they knew we would be going over this area with a fine tooth comb if we found a couple of dead kids here. I mean they left enough evidence here to have someone looking at it real serious. Do you think they didn't care if they got caught?"

"Who knows? It doesn't seem likely. If they didn't care, they sure went to a hell of a lot of trouble to make sure they covered this grave up carefully so it wouldn't be noticed." Philip's breath became more labored as he returned to the job at hand, "it just doesn't make sense."

"Here, let me take over for a while, Phil, before I have another body on my hands. You college types are not exactly suited for manual labor." With that, Kip jumped into the small hole.

"Thanks smartass, just for that you do the work." Philip sat down and leaned against the tree. "Didn't any of their friends know what they were doing down here?"

"Nope. I asked everyone the kids hung out with. They were good kids. One girl did suggest that maybe they came down her to bust their cherries, as she so delicately put it. It seems they had been dating for some time but never went all the way."

"You mean they were both virgins? Now that is a rare feat for kids this day and age."

"One thing did stick in my mind though, Bud's mother mentioned that he had a strange fascination with this place. I thought of you and your fascination with this place."

"You mean he was into history like me?"

"No, not really. According to his mom, there was no particular reason that she knew of. He just liked to hang around here. She thought he came here to unwind.

"Must be my turn by now," Philip said as he stood up to grab his shovel, but Kip was not ready to give up yet.

The digging was going a lot slower than they had figured and Philip decided it would be quicker to go back to town and get another shovel. Luckily, Martha had a spare at her house that she let him use, to plant his rose bush. This time he was going to drive, his back was killing him. When he got back, they made much quicker progress with both of them working. They had just reached about the six foot mark when they heard a thud. Both men, knowing they were nearing their destination, began to pick up the pace. When they uncovered their objective, they stood back and just stared at it, not knowing what to do. The only thing in the hole were the remains of an old, rotten, and quite empty coffin. Very little remained but one thing was perfectly clear, whoever had been buried there was absent now. Either that, or there had never been anyone there to begin with and that didn't seem like a real possibility. Filled with disappointment, the men silently filled back in the hole and put the sod back on top, this work went much quicker than the digging. By the time they were finished the last rays of sunlight were filtering through the trees.

"We did all this for nothing," Kip finally said.

"Did we?" questioned Philip. "At least there wasn't a fresh body down there."

"Jesus," Kip laughed, "I never even thought about that possibility. I guess it's possible that someone was burying something instead of digging something up. You're wasting your time being a teacher, you should be a detective. Anyway, you look beat, why don't you go home and get some rest."

"What about you, you're not exactly fresh as a daisy."

"I'm going to get some shut eye, too. We've done all we can do. Now it will be in the hands of the FBI. But first, I have to get something to eat."

When they got back to their cars, Philip threw his shovels in the trunk and got ready to go. "Call me."

"I will," came the reply from Kip who was getting into his own car. They had come looking for answers, but were leaving with more questions. If there had been a body in that hole, which the coffin would indicate, where was it? Although both men had the same thought, neither had said it aloud. They had had enough for one day.

Kip watched as Philip's car pulled away, and he was just getting ready to go himself when the oddest feeling came over him. Without thinking, he turned his gaze to the old manor on the hill. It was there. There was a reason he could not feel the fowl presence from his adolescence in the cemetery, it had moved. It was coming from the old manor. Kip tried to shrug it off but the feeling was not to be denied, it was getting stronger. It was the same feeling he had so many years ago in the cemetery. At first he was frozen with fear, it seemed to be drawing him. Then, swiftly the strange attraction turned into a challenge. Whatever lurked in the old manor was daring him to come. "This is stupid," Kip said out loud, "being haunted by a childhood fear, I'm a grown man for God's sake."

And still a coward, he thought he heard a voice say.

With that, he grabbed his flashlight out of the glove box and began walking up the hill toward the old manor. It was time he faced his own fears, real or imagined.

Sue walked up and down in front of Professor Parker's front walk. She would surprise him with the news that they were now officially neighbors. Then, when he asked her in for a drink, she would tell him just how she really felt about him. No more beating around the bush, she would just come right out with it. After all, he was a man and she was a woman, a very good-looking rich one, at that. She had never said so, but it was not her parents that were paying for her upcoming holiday. In fact, they very much wanted her to come home. They were not even paying her way through college, she was doing it all herself. When her dear grandmother, Lady Barkley passed away she surprised Sue, as well as a number of disgruntled relatives, by leaving the entirety of her nine-million-dollar estate to eight-year-old Sue. Unlike the rest of the family, Sue adored the woman, who was bedridden for the last two years of her life.

Sue visited every day, bringing her flowers and gifts, not because she was the family matriarch, but because Sue loved her dearly. The stories her grandmother would tell about her family coming to America without a penny to their name. How her father made his money smuggling booze from Canada during prohibition and used that money to start his own investment firm. She talked about the Second World War and how she had worked for the Red Cross.

Then there were the times she would put her fragile hands on Sue and convey the story of the man she loved and how she let him slip through her fingers. She had married the man her parents told her to wed, the man they said could best provide for her, a man of extreme wealth and influence, instead of the man she truly loved. She told Sue how much she had regretted this decision and sometimes, retelling this tale would bring tears to her eyes and Sue's heart would break. Now, standing in the cool night air for over an hour, she had made up her mind to spend every last dime if she had to, to get the man she loved.

Sue saw Philip's MG as it reached the outskirts of downtown. Smiling broadly with anticipation, she quickly slipped behind a tree for the big surprise. Just as she was ready to pop out, the MG turned to the right on Chestnut and then left on Maple, stopping directly across the street from her new home. Shit, she said to herself, she had been so ready, so excited, now that magic moment would have to wait. Slowly she walked back home, head hung low. Here he was, in front of Franky's house, the man she adored.

Philip came strolling out of the Lakes' front door just as Sue made the corner onto Maple. Behind him came Franky's mother. At his car, Philip turned and kissed her long and hard on the lips. Sue stopped dead in her tracks. It was plain to see that they were in love. Sue ran back around the corner and out of sight, hiding her face behind her purse. What a fool she had been, she ran hurriedly up the back steps to her apartment and turned just in time to see Professor Parker pull around the corner.

Kip walked silently up the last twenty feet of the path. At its end loomed the old mansion. Even in the dark, the touch of age was overwhelming. No one knew for sure just how old the place was, or why no one had ever bothered to tear it down or restore it. It was said the house was cursed. Every time someone even thought about tearing down the place, that person would meet with tragedy. The Gibsons, who actually owned the property, had been trying to sell the place for over twenty years but had not received even one decent offer.

The light from Kip's flashlight illuminated what remained of the back steps leading to an old stone terrace. For just a moment, Kip could picture it as it must have been when it was first built, the terrace filled with live ferns, stone statues everywhere and ladies in long flowing gowns dancing arm-in-arm with their gentleman friends. In its day, it must have been a real showcase. Now in the twilight, however, it seemed like an old man bent and weather-beaten. Kip thought of the poem he had learned in college, "Ozymandias," and how this house had much in common with the statue in the poem. Whoever had built this so long ago must have been quite powerful and his wealth almost unheard of for the times.

Kip crossed the terrace and walked up to the still-hanging French doors. Slowly, he opened them. At once, he was overwhelmed with a repugnant odor. Decomposing flesh, that is what he smelled. Once when he was young, his cat, Boots, had crawled into the root-cellar and died while the family was on vacation; it was the same smell at the Gibson's and the same smell here. The smell of rotting meat. Kip struggled with his inner fears and began to wonder if going there alone at night had been such a good idea. He felt as though he were walking straight into a trap.

Terror began to build deep in his thoughts and visions, a terror which he thought he left behind in childhood memories; they were taking a grip on his will. He wanted to run, to flee as he had that day at the cemetery. He was no longer Kip Gillmore, detective and defender of justice, but little Kippy the terrified little child.

"No," he yelled into the gloom, "not this time. I'm through running." He straightened his back, pushed back his childhood fears, and walked straight through the door of the house.

Kip found himself standing in what he assumed was a large ballroom. He had never seen a room this immense in Michigan houses. It had high ceilings, and in the dim light he saw what remained of the hardwood floors. Directly across from where he stood, a wide staircase split off to opposite wings of the house. On his left, was a fireplace, black and charred with age, proof in fact that at one time someone had made this place their home. On both sides of the door were enormous bookcases, and the solitary piece of furniture was an old rocker in front of the fireplace. On the right side of the room, moonlight glimmered where a portion of the wall had surrendered to age, and leaves and tree branches had fallen in.

Kip sighed, just another old house, an old empty house. This thought was short lived, however, when he felt an unfriendly gust of wind come from behind him. All at once, shadows seemed to dance before him, the endless tangles of webs began to sway. Everything in the house began to close in on him, the broken rocker, the bookshelves; even the staircase seemed to be growing toward him. Kip closed his eyes, biting back the fear. When he opened his eyes only a few seconds later the rocker was just inches away and without warning, it sailed through the air, barely missing his head, and smashed into the wall behind him. Kip's breath became shallow as a sturdier breeze rushed his back. Now he was having trouble keeping his balance, and one of the large bookcases came crashing down around his feet. Kip looked around trying to anticipate the next area of attack. Slowly, he started to back up to the French doors, knowing his only chance was to escape this house. The doors abruptly slammed themselves shut and then, just as suddenly, opened again. Over and over, the doors slammed and opened until Kip felt as if he were living in a hellish nightmare. Panic was taking a firm hold when suddenly, as if by a miracle, moonlight washed over the room. A cloud that had been covering the moon had passed by, permitting the light to come through the opening in the wall. Slowly he moved toward the opening, his eyes moving from the rocker to the remaining bookcase, then to the open doors. Suddenly, he heard a noise coming from over the fireplace. He turned all his attention there and saw a naked figure, practically human in form, slithering down the wall like a giant insect. It stopped for just a second and Kip thought he could hear it hissing at him. He could not make out a face, for which he was thankful. He turned and sprinted for the opening. This time, he did not look back. He heard the creature as it hit the floor, then heard the flop of its footsteps coming across the floor. It was gaining on him.

Kip leaped through the breach in the wall and landed on his side in a patch of ragweed. He heard a loud crack and at once was engulfed in pain. He knew he had broken at least one rib. Without hesitation, he grabbed his side and continued to run, losing his flashlight in his mad dash for safety. Blindly, he fled down an incline before tripping on a large stone. He landed head first on a pile of rocks. His head began to swirl with agony; he felt dizzy and blood was now flowing from his upper lip. Ascending to his knees, he turned and looked back. There was nothing there. From inside the house he caught the sound of laughter, wicked and evil. Again, he was taken aback by the flopping sound of those peculiar footsteps, getting close to the opening. Half running and half staggering, he made his way down the incline, certain the creature was close behind. He could see his car some twenty yards away and he tried to sprint the final distance, still holding his side. About five feet from safety, Kip stopped dead in his tracks. There, in front of the car, sat a stray Doberman Pinscher. Kip thought he had seen it earlier roaming around, and now here it was, sitting back on its haunches, baring its long, white fangs. Without warning, the dog bounded and Kip tried to cover his face from the attack. The dog, however had no interest in Kip and ran past him into the darkness. Kip ran for the car door and flung himself inside. Hastily he turned the ignition, and slammed the door shut. As the engine raced to life, he hit the lights, illuminating the darkness. In the brightness, he saw for only a split second, the figure of a huge man and at arm's length he held the still kicking dog by the throat. Kip sped away, made the turn on Michigan Avenue and headed toward Jackson. He never made it.

MONDAY

Franky awoke to the sound of his mother's laughter filtering up the stairs. Since he had heard his mother's invitation of the night before he assumed that Professor Parker had come for breakfast. He got dressed as quickly as possible and headed down the stairs but, instead of his mentor in the kitchen, he ran into his nemesis. Jake sat at the table eating a steaming bowl of oatmeal and looked up as Franky came into the room, fixing him with those large puppy-dog eyes.

"Hi hon." Martha said. "Want some breakfast?"

"No thanks, I'm not hungry."

"Hi Franky," said Jake, reaching out his hand.

"Hello," Franky answered, ignoring the outstretched hand and nodding his head instead.

The room remained silent until Martha could not stand it any longer. "Here, let me fix you something, it's what a mother lives for."

Franky made his way around to the opposite side of the table and sat facing Jake. "Just coffee please."

"Okay. After Jake is finished with breakfast maybe you can give him a hand unloading his stuff from the van. And that old bed of Gramma's needs to be brought up from the basement, too."

Franky grunted in response. He felt no need to encourage her in her enthusiasm.

Martha looked deeply into her cup of coffee, not wanting to see the reaction when she unloaded the next part on Franky. "Of course you'll have to clear out some space in your room before you bring the stuff up."

"My room?" Franky said too loudly for good manners, "What's wrong with the spare bedroom?"

"Didn't I tell you? I turned that into a sewing room about a week ago. I'm sure I told you that, didn't I?"

Franky knew he was being set up but didn't know how in the hell to get out of it. Still he was desperate to give it a shot. "Couldn't we clear that stuff out and . . ."

"Now you wait just a minute young man. I have been wanting my own sewing room since we moved into this place. It's my own little get-away and I have no intention of giving it up now. There is absolutely no reason why the two of you can't share a room." She had delivered this with all the motherly sternness that she could muster. "This is my final word on it," she finished and hoped it was good enough.

"Look, Aunt Martha," Jake stated in his deep clear voice, "if this is going to be a problem . . ."

"No problem at all, right Franky?" said Martha as she turned and gave a harsh look in Franky's direction.

One look into his mother's eyes told him all he needed to know: the subject was closed. "No, it's no problem, Mom."

To Franky it seemed that the invasion into his domain had taken no time at all. The bed had been moved and he was hauling the last load, a large sea chest, from the van to the house when Philip arrived just in time to hold the door.

"Good morning," he said from the doorway.

"I'm in the kitchen, Phil. Come on in."

Philip found his way to the kitchen where Martha was hard at work cleaning up after breakfast. "Sorry, I'm late. I overslept. Must be my body is going to enjoy spring break in spite of myself." The lie came smoothly for a man who seldom ever told one. In fact, Philip had not managed more than an hour or so of sleep in the last few nights. The vision of death hovered over him, waiting for the moment he began to sleep. It would drag him back into that world of horror where hooded devils devoured their living prey and blue eyed young men with blood stained faces reached out to steal his soul. He had even thought of calling to cancel breakfast, but the thought of seeing Martha and his unwillingness to disappoint her had given him a second wind and new-found strength.

"If you'll pardon me for saying so Philip, you look like shit."

Again, Philip was impressed with her powers of observation. He had thought he had done a good job of covering up the fact that he was half dead on his feet.

"Are you sick? Have you been having trouble sleeping?"

"As a matter of fact, I haven't been sleeping real sound."

"Don't you hate that? Then, it just kind of snowballs. The more tired you are, the worse you sleep until you feel like you're going to keel over. It happens to me once in a while, but I take a sleeping pill and it straightens me right out. I think I still have some if you want to try one."

"No," said Philip a little too quickly, causing Martha to give him a strange look. "I mean, no thanks, I just never use those things."

"Well, suit yourself, but they really do help me." With that, she proceeded to serve Philip breakfast consisting of a huge bowl of steaming oatmeal topped with brown sugar and milk, a plate of eggs over medium, hash-browns, two strips of bacon, two sausage patties and toast with homemade strawberry jam on the side.

"Good Lord woman, if I eat all of this, you will have to roll me out of the house," he said only half-joking.

"Eat what you can, maybe some good food in your stomach will help you sleep. I hope you don't mind, but I already ate with my nephew, Jake."

"It's my own fault for being late," answered Philip.

"Well, you're here now and after you eat, I want to introduce you to Jake."

"I sort of met him coming in. He sure is a good looking rascal isn't he?"

"I think so. He looks like his dad, that would be my brother Jonah."

"Personally, I think he looks a lot like his Aunt Martha, Phillip countered.

Upstairs, Franky and Jake were putting the finishing touches on the new living arrangements. Franky had never realized just how big his room was. Even the extra bed took up very little of the floor space including the oversized trunk at the end.

"You can have the dresser in the corner under the window. I don't use that one much. Most of my stuff is in here," Franky said, pointing to a large old-fashioned dresser with swinging doors.

"Great," Jake said looking at Franky's back. "I've missed you. How come you never came to visit us with your mom?"

Franky didn't know how to answer, so he just shrugged his shoulders.

"Look, Franky, if we don't clear the air right now, I don't know if we ever will. You're pissed at me about something and I don't know what it is."

"I'm not pissed," Franky growled, still refusing to look at Jake. "What have I got to be pissed about?"

"I don't know but this has been going on since we were kids. I love you like a brother, man, but I sure as hell don't understand you. This cold shoulder shit is driving me crazy."

Franky turned and looked his cousin in the eye, "I'm jealous," he said, honest with him for the first time.

"Jealous, of what?" asked Jake with surprise. He stopped putting his clothes away and sat on the edge of his bed to face his cousin head on.

"You get the looks, you get the girls, and you get every damn thing you want. What the hell did I ever get? Nothing, not a damn thing."

"I don't know what you think I got, buddy, but you need a reality check."

"Everything has always been so easy for Jake. The whole world revolves around you and you know it."

"Whose world, Franky, yours? God knows you're the only one that seems to have an issue."

"Fuck you."

"Come on, Franky. It hasn't been easy for either one of us. Remember, it was my dad sitting in the seat next to your dad when that plane went down. That made things tough for both of us."

"Shut up."

"Not this time, Franky. You've had your way all these years, and this time you are going to listen."

He grabbed Franky and pinned him to the bed. "If you want me to leave when I've had my say, I will. But now it's my turn."

"I want you out of here now." Franky shouted at the top of his lungs.

Downstairs Martha and Philip heard Franky's scream and Philip jumped to his feet.

"No," said Martha grabbing his wrist, "this is something they have to work out for themselves. Let's go for a short walk."

Philip gave her a confused look, but she just smiled and grabbed her purse.

"When our fathers died, you got weird, real weird," Jake said still sitting on top of Franky.

"Fuck you. Now get off." Franky struggled briefly but soon stopped as he realized Jake's bulk was too much for him. He lay still again.

"You say you're jealous of me, right?"

"How could I be jealous of a stuck up little prick like you?"

"Stuck up? You're the one who's stuck up. Don't you remember what it was like before the accident? We used to be close, the best of friends. Remember? But after the accident you wanted nothing to do with me, you treated my friends like shit and you always acted like an ass whenever I was around.

You played the part of the poor little boy who had lost his daddy so the world owed you something special. Well it doesn't. You have to quit feeling sorry for yourself and get on with your life."

"Like you did? Well maybe it was easier for you. I loved my dad."

Jake's cheeks flushed a scarlet red, and he raised his fist over Franky's unprotected face. Franky closed his eyes and tried to prepare himself for the blow.

"No, oh no. That's too easy. That would give you the reason you want to hate me. You are jealous of me. Jealous because I didn't dig a hole and pull the dirt in on top of me like you did. Because I didn't die like you did when our dads died. I did it the hard way, pal. I suffered, and I grieved, and then I moved on." Jake had started sobbing and the snot ran down his upper lip. "I did it the hard way because I did it alone. Night after night crying myself to sleep, nightmares of that plane coming down playing over and over in my head, the look on my Dad's face when . . ."

Jake paused and took a long deep breath.

"The one person I needed was you. You were the only one who could understand, the only one who could know what it felt like, but you shut me out, man, and that made it hurt even more. All these years we could have been helping each other."

Slowly, Jake got up and walked over to the dresser he had just filled and started to empty it back into his chest. "I still could use someone like you to talk to; there are times that I have a hard time dealing, man."

After a while, Franky got up and wiped his nose on the back of his hand. "I'm sorry. I never knew. I guess I couldn't see past my own hurt to see what it was doing to you. I wish it could have been different."

"Don't worry about it." Jake said, never turning around.

"I wanted to do things with you, to confide in you, but I didn't know how. I still don't know how really, but I want to try." Franky pulled his hair behind his ears. "I don't hate you, you're my cousin, and I love you. I want you to stay."

Jake stopped packing and looked at Franky. "If you mean that, I will. I really would like to stay."

"I do," Franky said and then smiled.

While Franky and Jake were having words, Father McMurry sat in his office. The morning light that filtered through the stained glass window illuminated the room in brilliant arrays of color. This was his room, the only place left for him to hide away from the rest of the world and enjoy the sweet touch of silence. In this room, he was safe and secure and closer to God. But this morning, his heart was very heavy. Surely, this manuscript was the work of a mad man. Even the way it was written, as if parts had been taken out to protect the innocent. No one in his right mind could have dreamed up a tale like this and expect anyone else to believe it, certainly no one in the Church, he knew he could always call Rome or even his own Bishop for confirmation, but he was afraid they would think he was a raving lunatic for even asking, and rightfully so.

He got up and walked over to the door, but not before giving one more glance back at the manuscript and the ancient book that sat next to it. The author of the manuscript had made it sound so believable. You could almost trust that he had lived through the terror, as he claimed. It was clear from the author that he believed every word he wrote. Father McMurry kept telling himself it was impossible but part of him, a hefty part from somewhere deep in his heart, couldn't dismiss it. It was that damn book. It was evil; he could feel it. He said he would read both works, and he tried. But every time he even got near that book, his hands trembled and sweat broke out all over his body. If it was truly what the good Father claimed in his manuscript, then it should never be read, not even by a man of God.

As for Officer Gillmore, he would tell him nothing. If in fact Gillmore came back and asked for his assistance he would know why. And if he did, God help him, God help them all.

As the conversation died, a disquieting silence took its place. Both Jake and Franky were feeling a little awkward about what had taken place and were unsure of how they were supposed to act now. Then out of the blue, Franky whispered, "I have a crush on this girl." He did not really comprehend why he had said it, but once it was out, it felt good to confide in somebody for a change.

"Really?" said Jake, "Who? Do I know her?"

"No," answered Franky, suddenly doubting if he had done the right thing.

"Well, come on, details, tell me about her."

"Her name is Sue, Sue Barkley. I have a class with her at P.U."

"Have you asked her out yet? Did she say yes, no, maybe?"

"Are you kidding, she's beautiful. No way, I have trouble even talking to her, let alone asking her out. She wouldn't want to go out with me. I'm a dweeb."

"Stand up."

Franky stood up, and Jake led him to the mirror on the small dresser he had just put his clothes back into. He grasped Franky's long stringy red hair and pulled it back behind his head. He said, "Franky, you are not a bad looking guy, but look at this mop. No one has worn their hair like this since the sixties. And no one has had a wardrobe like yours since the fifties."

"Hey man, I pick out my own clothes."

"Well then, all your taste must be in your mouth. But now, you have come to the professor of style and all you have to do is put yourself in my hands. Just trust me," he said with a grin.

"I don't know about this."

"Come on, I still got a thousand bucks stuck away that Mom gave me for an emergency. Believe me this qualifies."

"But . . ."

"But nothing," said Jake. "We'll take the van into J-town and by the time we get back this Sue Burney . . ."

"Barkley," corrected Franky.

"Burney, Barkley, whatever. She won't be able to keep her pretty little hands off you."

"Yeah, sure."

"Didn't I tell you to trust me?"

"Okay, okay, but I'm bushed. What say we do this after I get some snooze time in?"

"Are you kidding? You want to take a nap, now, when there is so much we could be doing, all the trouble we could be causing?"

"I'm serious as a train wreck," he said stifling a yawn. "I was up all night watching TV."

In reality, Sue was up all night watching TV with Franky observing her through his bedroom window.

"If you insist. Come to think of it, a nap doesn't sound like a bad idea. I got up at five this morning to get here early." He stretched out on his bed and then gave Franky, a wicked grin, "We haven't done this since we were ten."

Franky laughed and lay down on his bed. "Do you still snore like a fucking bull?"

"Yes, do you still pee the bed?"

"Yes, but only after an all-night bender."

"Right, like you've ever had an all-night bender."

"Well then, there's your answer. Now shut up, I'm trying to sleep.

"Fuck this, I'm going to get something to drink, we'll leave after you get your beauty sleep, and trust me, you need it." With that, he was up and gone.

Franky smiled. Somehow, he knew his life was changing for the better. The last thing he heard before sinking into sleep was his mom and Professor Parker returning from their walk.

After a cup of coffee and twenty minutes of conversation, Martha looked at Philip across the table and said, "Philip, go home."

"Was it something I said?" Philip questioned.

"You look beat, go home and take a nap."

"Really, I'm fine."

"You're not fine, but I want you to be fine tonight. You and I have a date and I want you in good shape. You are still picking me up aren't you?"

"I sure am."

"Good. Then get your ass home and get some sleep. I have to get some work done around here, anyway. This is the last day of my vacation and I like getting all the stuff done I need to do so I can enjoy the rest of it. So, you get home and build up your strength, you may just need it later."

Philip grinned. The message was coming through loud and clear. "Alright, I can take a hint." He got up and kissed her softly on the cheek and found his own way out.

Outside the sun was hot, it was going to be a real scorcher. It felt nice to be happy again and looking forward to the evening. Who was he kidding? He was as excited as a school kid looking forward to the prom. He kept wondering how the night would go, and if it could possibly turn out as great as he hoped it would.

It was only a short walk to his house, but about half-way home he was utterly exhausted. Odd how it came over him so fast, but then again, going without sleep for so long was guaranteed to take a toll on you sooner or later. He had never felt so tired, so much so that when he got home he stripped out of his clothes and flung himself on the bed not even concerned if he dreamed. All he wanted to do was snooze, after all even a bad slumber was better than no slumber, wasn't it?

Within minutes he felt himself slipping away into unconsciousness, and then the nightmare continued as if it were a video he had turned off in the middle.

He was back in the field. Fritz was gone, but Philip could still feel his presence close at hand. It was as if he were observing from a far off place.

From the center of the clearance, he heard a brash crackling noise. Philip turned just in time to see a huge flame leap up from the fire pit. He started toward it slowly, no longer afraid of being seen; after all, this was his dream and even now, he was aware that it was all happening in his sleep. A soldier who had been in on the raid passed in front of him as if he were invisible. It seemed that these bizarre people from the past were completely unaware of him. Philip questioned if you could feel warmth in dreams because the closer he got to the fire he could feel the warmth from the flames on his face. He also grasped that contrary to popular belief, he was dreaming in color, the flames were a bright red and yellow. He tucked all this information in the back of his mind, telling himself he would think about it when he woke up. He was closer to the fire now, consumed by the flame. Just a few more feet and he would just walk right into it. He wondered if the flame could burn him if he did. His surroundings became a blur until the single thing that remained was the fire and a man on the ground bent over next to it. It was the priest and he was praying.

"One more is all Father," came a voice from the haze.

"Throw him in," the priest instructed.

From behind him a hooded figure came soaring through the air and landed squarely in the flames. The fire exploded once again as the priest kept repeating his incantations. There was a scream of agony, and then only the whisper of the priest's prayers in Latin could be heard.

"Father, we only found eleven," came the voice from the haze.

The priest raised his head and made the sign of the cross before rising. He brushed the dirt off his knees as his eyes swept the area. "The two that fled must be found. They cannot get away, do you understand? Find them and bring them back to me alive. They must be burned with prayer. If they are strong enough to get away from you so easily, they must have the powers of a high priest. They will be dangerous so be cautious. Remember to pray. Any weakness in your faith will be your doom. We can only hope it is not too late." As the priest had spoken, the flames had begun to fade and now even the priest had begun to lose form. As he did so, he aged, from a younger man to a very old one.

Finally, nothing remained but complete and total darkness. In the darkness, a voice he knew to be the shadow creature began to speak. "Find him, for he lives. It is Fritz you seek here. Find him." Philip realized that the priest and the shadow creature were the same presence, they had the same voice. He felt someone else, other than the priest, take his hand in the darkness. He was no longer unaccompanied and his soul was reassured by the touch. From the obscurity came the plea once more: "find him."

"Wake up, man!" shouted Jake. "You have been out for three hours. Man, when you said you needed a nap, you weren't kidding."

Franky sat on the side of his bed and looked around with a dazed look. Jake was already heading for the door and said over his shoulder, "Come on man, we've got shopping to do."

Franky continued to sit on the bed for a minute trying to shake off the sleep and then got up to follow Jake out the door, feeling like a lamb being led to the slaughter.

For the next three hours, he was dragged from one store to another. Any place that even looked like it might carry men's clothing was investigated from top to bottom in spite of Franky's protest. He assumed putting together a new wardrobe would be easy, a few pair of jeans and some shirts, but Jake was not an easy man to satisfy. Every time Franky picked out something, Jake would shake his head and say, "looks like shit" or "that looks queer." So, he continued to drag poor Franky from one store to another and one dressing room after another, spending more time to pick out one shirt than Franky had ever spent in a store for anything.

Finally, after combing the Sagebrush store in front of Meijer, Jake was satisfied and more than eager to check out his handy work. He declined to tell Franky exactly how much he had spent for outfitting him, but Franky guessed that they had taken a good sized chunk out of the money Jake's mother had given him. Every time Franky had tried to pay for anything, Jake would simply stand in his way. But clothes shopping was not going to be the end of it for Franky, Jake still had other alterations in mind.

It was around six by the time they got home, and Martha was just walking in from getting her things done when they pulled in the drive. "Well, how did it go?" she asked Jake.

"Not bad, Aunt Martha, not bad at all," laughed Jake, "A bit like pulling teeth, but I think we got the job done." He turned and headed up the walk.

Just then Franky got out of the van and Martha's smile was so broad that it highlighted her entire face. Franky said nothing; he stood there with a panicky look on his face. His hair was gone. For the first time in ten years, Martha could clearly see her son's face. The transformation was incredible. His hair was still cut longer but the long stringy look was absent. He looked normal, not as much like a nerd. In fact, he was very decent looking. He had left the house a boy, and had come back looking like a man. Like the man she had fallen in love with many years ago, his father, Frank Sr.

If a haircut had made that much difference, Martha couldn't wait to see what the new garments would add to the total picture.

For the next half-hour Franky was made to parade around in his new jeans, (Lees, Males, and even a pair of Jordash), dress pants, sweaters, sport shirts, dress shirts and even new shoes and socks. Even though Franky was doing this under protest, he stopped at the top of the stairs while going down to display his last ensemble and observed himself in the mirror. He couldn't believe the difference himself. Jake actually knew what he was doing. He had never thought of himself as being sexy in any way, but he had to admit that with the right covering, even he had a certain appeal that was lacking under the outdated rags he wore. However, he didn't know if he had what it took to pull off this look. He felt naked, exposed. He could clearly see the knob of his cock in his jeans and they were riding right up the crack of his ass. He wasn't sure he could go out in public like that. What if people laughed? This might be the eighties, but Franky wasn't sure if he was ready for it. Even more important was his hair, or lack thereof. He kept reaching up to pull it back only to realize it was gone. How could he have let Jake talk him into this? This morning he was the same old Franky, contentedly hating his cousin, thankfully living in his own little time warp. Now, he had made up with his cousin, had let Jake drag him into this decade, even telling him his deepest secrets. This was not how he had planned the day when he got up this morning. Again, he reached up to pull his hair back. Abruptly a picture from the Peanuts cartoon flashed into his mind: Linus, holding his blanket up to his ear with his thumb stuck in his mouth. "Fuck it," he said out-loud as he began to dance in front of the mirror. "I look good and it's time I started feeling good." With that, he turned and headed down the stairs.

Martha was more than a little pleased by what she had seen, especially the dress pants, shirt and tie.

While Sally Smith still lay in a coma, two doors down lay Kip Gillmore. The events of the previous night were at best a blurred memory in the overwhelming cloud of pain-relieving drugs. Agent Bibens from the FBI had tried to get a statement but he wasn't sure what had happened, except that he thought he had seen what he perceived to be the devil with deep blue eyes and he sure as hell was not going to tell the FBI that. Maybe it was all a dream. After all, he had let himself get a little carried away with all that satanic shit.

"Anybody home?" asked a familiar voice from the doorway.

Kip looked up and saw Philip as he walked the rest of the way into his room, his eyes full of disbelief.

"The doc said I could only stay a minute." Philip said as he made his way to the side of Kip's bed. "Is there anything I can get for you? Some water maybe."

Kip shook his head no. His entire face was battered, and he had a small row of stitches running across his chin.

"What the hell happened? They said you passed out behind the wheel and ran your car up a tree, but you looked fine when I left you and I'm damn sure you weren't drunk."

"I don't know, I think it was the knock on my head. I was in bad shape before I even got into my car. That much I recall. I told the FBI I was attacked down by the lake on a routine check." Kip started to say more but the effort sent a jolt of pain to his brain, and he felt faint. Besides having a hairline fracture to his jaw and a cut chin, he also had four broken ribs, a bump on the head, and a minor concussion. He closed his eyes until the discomfort passed. The only real injury he acquired in the crash was a bruised shoulder when it hit the steering wheel.

"That's okay, don't try to talk if it hurts. By the way there is a ton of cops out there and this guy named Bibens wasn't going to let me in at all."

"What did you tell him?" mumbled Kip.

"I told him I was an old friend, that's all."

"Did you tell him about the cemetery?"

"No. I told you, I didn't tell him anything about that."

"Good," said Kip, trying to pull himself into a sitting position. Philip seeing his struggle, tried to help but when he took his arm, Kip let out a low moan.

Once adjusted, Kip looked at Philip and said. "I went up to the manor after you left. The last thing I remember was walking up the hill. That and . . ." Kip looked away.

"And what?" Philip asked.

"And seeing this thing. It's burned into my memory. Look, I know this is going to sound crazy but it looked like, I don't know, it looked like a zombie or something. It was a man, but it looked like a walking corpse. Its skin just kind of hung there on the bone, and its skull was covered with pure white skin. No meat, just skin. It had these paper-thin lips, red as blood, with serrated teeth. But oh, it's eyes. The eyes were so beautiful, so blue."

Philip gasped and looked at Kip. He had seen Fritz. How in the hell was that possible. Fritz was just a dream, a nightmare of his own making.

"What's wrong?" Kip asked.

"Nothing" Philip answered. "Maybe those pain killers are making you come up with this stuff. Why don't we talk about it later, when you feel a little better?"

Kip was so fatigued from trying to talk that he agreed with him and lay back down. He could tell that Philip was distressed about something and wasn't telling all he knew.

"I've got to get going, but I'll be back up later to see you."

"One more thing before you take off," Kip said, hoping this piece of news might get Philip to offer more information, "I talked to Sam a little while ago."

"Sam, the coroner?"

"Yeah, he came up to tell me something weird was going on with the Cooper boy's body."

Philip looked at Kip.

"Could you look into that for me?"

"Sure, but how can I . . ."

"Don't worry. I told him you were coming and that you were secretly helping with the case. Sam's a good guy, he'll keep it under wraps. If what I think is going on, really is, then the FBI would only laugh at us. Stay away from them until we know for sure."

"What do you think is going on?"

"I'll let you know that when you come to take me home."

"Is that a bribe?"

"Sort of. The doc said if my test comes back okay, then I can go home as early as Wednesday, and I no longer have a car, remember."

"I'll be glad to pick you up, but can't you fill me in now?"

Kip had no idea what to tell him because he didn't have a clue himself. He was hoping to get Philip to tell him what he knew. Since he had no answer, he simply disregarded the question, rolled over and shut off the light.

Outside the hospital the spring breeze felt sharp on Philip's face. It was getting colder and a chill sunk down into his bones and lodged there. He heard the cry of a bird overhead, and the sound filled him with dread. As he made his way across the parking lot to the MG that stood unaccompanied in the sea of blacktop, he thought of the first night he started remembering his dreams and the shadow creature that lured him from his bed. He knew it was nothing more than a dream, but what was happening in Parksville was not. From deep inside him came the knowledge that the two were in fact connected. How that was true, he didn't know. But those bright beautiful blue eyes that Kip had seen were the eyes of Fritz. The same blue eyes he had gotten lost in. Philip could not get the vision of them out of his mind. "But why me?" he thought. "What do I have to do with all this?" Philip didn't realize he was talking out loud to the night air. His head was swirling with thoughts and wild imaginings, but of one thing he was certain: if he had seen Fritz, even in a dream, then Fritz had seen him, and there was no way out. The connection was made and the most he could do was try to save himself and the people that he cared about.

On the drive home, Philip had concluded that the answers could only come through his dreams. The idea of leaving himself open to another confrontation with Fritz terrified him, but he knew there was no other way to solve the problem. It helped a little to know he had friends in the dream-world to protect him. The priest and the shadow creature were one in the same, and it was the priest that had shown him what he had seen. He had taken him back in time to the beginning, to show him what had happened long ago. Maybe he appeared as the shadow creature because that was now his only true form. He didn't know if there was any truth in his speculations, but somehow he did know that he was not alone in this. Someone else, someone like himself, had been pulled into this mess, too. He wanted to know—had to know— who that other person was.

Upon arriving home, he regretfully called Martha and canceled their date. He told her he was too tired and after seeing him in the shape he was in that morning, she never questioned him. Instead she once again offered a sleeping pill and this time he accepted. After a few moments, she arrived at his door with the pill. They talked only for a few moments. After he had taken the pill and she was sure he was going straight to bed, Martha let herself out.

Philip walked into his bedroom, not bothering to get undressed, and lay down on his bed. Hopefully, he would soon have his next and final meeting with the shadow creature.

Sue Barkley had not left her apartment all day. She felt empty and alone. All of her dreams were now shattered at the discovery of Professor Parker's other woman. Since she had witnessed that kiss, she had been in a near daze. She wasn't used to not having everything she wanted, and she wanted Professor Parker. She thought of fighting for him and had even considered breaking into his house and waiting for him naked on his bed. However, common sense won out, and she realized that doing that could possibly drive the man away from her, still. She was not going to give up so easily, there must be something she could do. After all, what did that other woman have that she did not.

TIC, TIC, TIC,

Sue sat up straight and looked around for the sound.

TIC, TIC, TIC,

It was coming from the bedroom window, but all she could see from her seat on the bed was empty sky. Slowly she got up and made her way across the bedroom. Looking out the window she still saw nothing. She turned the latch and began to open it, but as soon as the window started to move, she saw the fingers clinging to the window seal. Looking down she saw a man climbing on all fours up the side of the house. Sue screamed and slammed the window back down hard on the curled white claw.

The scream that followed echoed in her ears. Quickly she opened the window again and the hand withdrew sending the man crashing to the ground. It took her a minute to get the courage to look down and when she did there was nothing there. She had expected to see him sprawled out on the ground, maybe with a broken neck or something, but there was nothing. She nearly jumped out of her skin when someone knocked on the door.

"You all right, honey? I heard a scream," came Mrs. Cartwright's voice through the door.

Sue, still shaking in terror managed a reply, "Yeah, I think so. Hold on." She grabbed a robe to cover her skimpy teddy and ran to the door. She unlocked it and opened it ready to throw herself into the comfort of Mrs. Cartwright's arms.

There, in the doorway stood a large figure. Its eyes shone with the glow of satisfaction. The first thing she noticed was the claw like hand she had slammed in the window. It was bent backwards at the knuckles.

Sue screamed, but in a flash, the creature had covered her mouth with its crippled hand and pushed her into the living room and onto the sofa.

When it released her, Sue started to scream again but when she looked into his bright blue eyes, the scream died in her throat and she began to feel calmer. Her entire body began to relax and every muscle seemed to become immobile. Its face was a mixture of rotted skin and flesh. In places, it looked almost normal, as if it were trying to heal itself. Half its teeth looked like those on a shark and some appeared to be human. Sue was beyond noticing, she was immersed in the deep blue eyes.

Slowly, he undid her robe, Sue did not move. Next, he grabbed the middle of her teddy and with a nail from his claw sliced it to expose her smooth young belly. He smiled an evil grin through his thin red lips and bent over.

Though Sue could feel his hot breath on her skin, she offered no resistance, he was still looking at her with those eyes.

Just then, a door downstairs slammed shut. This time, the real Mrs. Cartwright had returned, and as the creature turned to look at the door, it broke the hold he had on Sue. It only took a second but it was long enough. Instinct took control and Sue bashed her right leg into the monsters groin. He fell away grabbing at himself.

Sue jumped up and ran for the door. She was almost there when the creature sank his right claw deep into her calf. Her weight shifted and she slammed head first into the door.

The creature stood up, again displaying his hideous grin. He was enjoying this immensely.

He began to slink towards her like a cat ready to pounce on its prey.

Sue knew better than to look into its eyes again. She kept her eyes down and began to back away. Suddenly, her hand felt something behind her. The other day, when she had moved in, it had taken both hands to lift the large porcelain dog, but now with one hand she hurled it around with a swing that would have left Babe Ruth green with envy. It hit the monster squarely in the forehead and shattered into a million pieces. The blow sent it rolling across the floor, and it landed with a loud thud by the door. Sue quickly got up and looked for something to use to finish him off. There was no reason to scream now; she could hear Mrs. Cartwright running up the stairs. The only thing Sue wanted now was to kill this thing.

In a flash, the creature was on his feet again, large pieces of porcelain protruding from his forehead. Sue gave a swift kick to his groin area again but this time it did not even flinch. The amusement had gone out of his face, he was no longer enjoying the chase. Slowly, it moved toward her, a hiss escaping between its clamped lips. Sue backed up, unaware that she was going through the bedroom door. She found herself looking at his face and was almost transfixed by his eyes again when she caught herself and looked away.

The creature, seeing that its power had again eluded her, started to run at her. Sue screamed and turned to run. She caught her foot on her grandmother's rocking chair and went head first into the bedroom window.

From outside in the hall Mrs. Cartwright was pounding on the door and calling her name, but Sue didn't notice. She fell to the floor, blood gushing from her scalp. Still she could see him coming at her. In desperation, she stood and with every ounce of energy she had left, she swung.

The creature simply moved out of the way of the blow and curling his broken claw into a fist, sent it flying into Sue's mid-section. Sue buckled and staggered to the broken window. This time there was nothing to stop her momentum, and she went straight through the opening. She grabbed for the windowpane, but the broken and jagged glass severed a finger from her right hand. She held on for a moment and then fell without a sound.

The creature, realizing what it had done reached out to grab her but it was too late. She landed on the cellar door and bounced off into the grass.

The creature now heard the turning of a key in the lock. He hissed at the door and scurried out the window. When his feet hit the ground he ran over to where Sue lay and rolled her over. It was too late, she was dead and no good to him now. He hissed again and disappeared into the night.

Tuesday

Jake was awakened by the sound of sirens. The room was filled with red and white flashing lights. His first thought was that the house was on fire and no one had bothered to tell him. He flew from his bed and to the small double pane window which faced the front of the house.

There were two cop cars and an ambulance in front of Mrs. Cartwright's house. Quietly, he stood watching the commotion below as the police and medics scrambled around to the back of the house. Mrs. Cartwright appeared on her front porch. She was weeping.

Jake reached over and gave Franky a shake but he simply rolled over, oblivious to the world around him.

Jake pulled on his jeans and tee-shirt and gave Franky one last shake as he left out the door. How could anyone sleep that soundly? He walked out the door and down the steps to the front door.

By the time Jake hit the front steps of Mrs. Cartwright's porch, a policeman had already caught sight of him and told him to move back.

"Please let him by," pleaded Mrs. Cartwright, "he is a very dear friend of mine."

He was then allowed to pass and upon reaching Mrs. Cartwright, was held in a long embrace.

"Oh, Jakey, Oh Jakey," sobbed Mrs. Cartwright onto the boys shoulder, obviously near hysteria.

Jake held her tight without a word.

"I don't know how this could of happened," she ranted, "I saw the sign and did nothing."

Around the corner came the medics carrying a stretcher. The body under the blood stained-sheet lay with its face covered. Jake was sure who ever it was, was dead. Still the men moved with all the speed they could to load it into the back of the ambulance. Gradually, one by one, the policemen also made their way to the front as well.

By this time, Mrs. Cartwright had regained some of her composure. Jake led her inside the house and into her living room. Once there, he sat her down on the sofa and held her hand. All the while, she continued to babble. The only thing he made out clearly was the name Susan, poor girl, and something that sounded like, "bird, black bastard."

A man entered the room and identified himself as Captain Bibens of the FBI. He asked Jake to please leave the room for a moment, he wanted to talk to Mrs. Cartwright in private. Jake politely excused himself and walked into the kitchen only after Mrs. Cartwright gave a nod of assurance.

Once in the kitchen, Jake put on the water to boil; coffee sounded good to him, and needing a break, he sat down at the old oak table Mrs. Cartwright had brought back with her from New Orleans. Jake was quite surprised to see the house in this good of shape. He remembered when he was young, how run down the place had been. Maybe the reason it stuck out so much was the fact that back then all the houses on Chestnut were rather pleasant, except for this one. But then again, it had always looked bad on the outside but inside cozy and warm.

Susan, I wonder if she meant Franky's Susan, the one he is so crazy about. It must be, hadn't he told him that she rented an apartment from Mrs. Cartwright? His mind began racing with ideas of what had happened. Did she kill herself? Was she murdered? Until this spring, that thought would not have entered his mind. But those three sets of killings were the biggest thing ever to hit this town. The news keeps talking about it over and over again, and there was a strict curfew in effect.

Jake was finishing making a cup of coffee when a voice came filtering in from the other room. You can come back in now, son.

As Jake entered the room he found Mrs. Cartwright once again weeping. She was shaking all over and had gone pale.

"I am going to leave now, but I will be back in the morning," said Bibens coldly. "Please try and take it easy, there will be some officers outside for some time, and an officer will be stationed just up the road for the rest of the night."

Jake gave the man a mean glare. He did not know what was said while he was gone but could not believe the man had upset her; the agent sounded sincere, but to Jake his words came out cold and his condolences empty.

"I am going to notify the girl's parents as soon as I can. Lock your doors and do not let anyone in."

Mrs. Cartwright nodded in agreement.

"Good night then," he added and walked toward the door. Before he left, however, he gave a glance Jake's way, "By the way, you did not happen to see anything around here tonight did you?"

Jake shook his head, "No, the lights woke me up."

Bibens, giving no response, turned and walked out.

Before doing anything else, Jake walked over to the phone and dialed the Lakes' house. He was not at all sure if he could handle this by himself. Mrs. Cartwright did not look at all well.

Martha Lake heard the phone ring. At first she imagined it was a part of her dream. She began to wake, coming back to life. Her hand reached across the nightstand and found the receiver.

"Hello," she spoke in a faint voice.

"Aunt Martha, this is Jake."

"Jake is in bed, can you call back in the morning?"

"No this is Jake, Aunt Martha," came the reply.

"Jake," Martha said, her mind clearing. "Where are you?"

"I am over at Mrs. Cartwright's. Can you come over here please? There has been . . . an accident."

Martha sat up straight in her bed and her eyes flew open, she looked over at the small desk alarm clock that sat on the night stand next to the phone, it was 1:00 a.m.

"What's wrong honey, are you okay, is Mrs. Cartwright all right?"

"Yes, we are all right, but I would really like for you to come over as quick as possible. I will explain it when you get here. At least the little I know."

"I'll be right there. You just give me a minute."

"Thanks Aunt Martha," said Jake and hung up the phone.

Martha did not waste much time getting dressed. She simply slipped her jacket over her pajamas. She then grabbed her slippers and headed down the stairs.

She at once noticed the police car in front of Mrs. Cartwright's house. As she crossed the street, she could feel the watchful eyes of the officers inside. She wasted no time making her way up to the house. For the life of her, she could not figure out what was happening. Mrs. Cartwright had always been such a dear friend.

Jake was the one who opened the door and at once, Martha could see the look of concern on his face. He removed her jacket, as Martha entered, and hung it on the old fashion coat rack that stood by the door.

There sat Mrs. Cartwright, on the sofa, she was deathly pale, and Martha could never remember her looking so old.

"Martha," said Mrs. Cartwright, "you didn't have to come over."

"Now, you just never mind that Brandy," answered Martha.

Martha went and sat beside the nervous old lady and put her arm around her, she could feel her trembling and was aware of the way she continuously wrung her hands, her boney knuckles showing a dull white.

"Jake, go make us some tea, will you hon?" Martha asked in her take-charge voice. She knew she would have to have time alone with Mrs. Cartwright to calm her. As soon as Jake left the room Martha looked at the teary-eyed woman. She had always looked up to her. Martha had admired her for her strong nature, the way she had moved here in the sixties at the age of fifty, all by herself, a widow and managed to get along for all these years on her own. As far as Martha knew, she had no family. To make it even worse, were the rumors that after her husband had died at an early age, she had made her way down to New Orleans Red Light District, that she had run a whorehouse and that was where she got her money. True or not, it never mattered to Martha. "We all make it in this world the best we can and only God in heaven could pass the final judgment." That was her response to people who had tried telling her the story. Brandy Cartwright had always walked with her head held high and ignored the whispers of others, which is not so easy in a small town were gossip is a way of life.

"Now Brandy, I want you to take it slow and tell me what happened from beginning to end."

Mrs. Cartwright began to speak, her chin quivering. "I've seen the sign Martha, but I ignored it."

"What are you talking about Brandy?"

"The bird, the black devil that was in my house this afternoon. It's a sign of death Martha, and I just ignored it."

"Death," said Martha, "did someone die?"

Mrs. Cartwright burst out into tears.

Philip lay in his bed unaware of the commotion on the next street over. Nothing was left of this world for him, he had made the transfer into the world that he feared. Images began to float in and out of his mind, freely. The foreboding moon cast its eerie light through the glass window of his bedroom and there, he had seemed to become an imaginary character in an unsettling play.

Big Bill had simply walked through the far wall of his room and sat at the foot of his bed, as so many times he had done on his front porch. His hair was still wet and dripping in his eyes, his bibs were tattered and torn, but at least they covered the spot where Bill's guts had once been, that gave some comfort to Philip, though he knew he should have been terrified. He knew he was dreaming and even the blue complexion of Bill's skin did not shake him; after all, he was dead, what color would one expect.

"Hi ya, Teach," said Bill pulling on the straps of his bibs.

"Well, hello Bill," answered Philip trying to act as natural as possible.

"I look pretty shitty, don't I? That bastard snuck up on me, that's what he did, you got to get him for me Teach, ya hear? You gotta get that cocksucker for me."

"Just tell me what to do, Bill," answered Philip, setting up in his bed. "Just tell me what to do."

"It's cold here, Teach. Real cold."

Philip reached out to him, "Tell me what to do Bill."

In an instant, Bill had disappeared but Philip could still hear him far away in the distance, "So fucking cold here."

No sooner had Bill departed than the kids from the cemetery came through the wall. For a moment, Philip had the notion that somehow, he had opened the gateway to hell, and it ran right through his bedroom wall. Both stood there in complete silence, neither uttering a word. Philip knew at once who they were from the photos.

"Can I help you?" asked Philip.

There was no reply, only empty stares from eyes that seemed to plead for mercy. Their pain and sorrow was evident and finally Philip had to look away.

By the time he looked back they too had vanished, but this was not the end. Next came the Gibsons. Mrs. Gibson smiled broadly at Philip, the way she always did and Philip could tell she did not have in her teeth. The memory of how he had last seen her, the grotesque way this beast had used her body, came rushing upon Philip like a runaway truck.

"Oh, my God, I am so very sorry."

"Now dear," she spoke holding her husband's hand. "You have got to put an end to this thing." As she spoke, her head tilted to one side and the crease in her neck widened. Philip was sure her head would tumble off, but it didn't.

"How? Just tell me how."

Mr. Gibson held out his hands, the anguish in his face was overwhelming. Philip reached out to him, but they were both gone.

Philip lay back down, fear had finally begun to set in, voices were crying out in his ears, "Help us please, it's not fair, get that bastard, we did not mean to start this. I am so frightened my dear, it's so fucking cold."

As soon as it all started, everything stopped, and in the dim light, he sat alone. Endless emotions swept through him for the pain and suffering of these poor lost souls.

Then came a whisper, "Hi, Professor."

Philip turned, slowly, and in his bed next to him lay Susan. Philip at once began to cry. This was it, the straw that broke the camel's back, the push that would send him over the edge. He was going crazy and nothing could stop it.

"It's all right she spoke," unlike the others, there was no pain in her voice, she seemed happy, content, and her body had a beautiful glow that shone through the darkness. "I was one of the lucky ones. You see I got away. Soon, I will go to a better place, a delightful place, as well as the others if you can help them. They are trapped here and only you can set them free." With that, her form began to fade.

"No, please don't go, tell me what to do."

"Good-bye, Mr. Parker," she said, still fading. "I did love you, you know." And with that she was gone.

Everything was happening so fast that Philip felt drained. He had seen some very dear friends in their greatest hour of need, but still did not have a clue as to how to reassure them. Why had they come to me, why me? Questions, questions, he had come willingly to this dream to find answers, but all that he got were more questions.

"Will someone please let me know what the hell is going on here," he yelled into the night.

From the corner of his eye Philip caught a glimpse of a shadow moving across the floor. It climbed the same wall that only moments before had served as a doorway for the dead. There was just enough light to make it out, otherwise he would have missed it altogether.

"Well," said Philip with all the courage he could muster, "you're finally here. Now maybe, I can get some answers."

The shadow began to take form, Philip gasped as the face began to protrude from the wall. Suddenly an arm reached out into the open air, then a foot, within a second, a large man walked out from the wall and stood in front of Philip. Light began to flow from the creature's eyes as it came near; it had the same glow that he had seen on Susan. Philip pulled a blanket over his face.

"Look at me," said the creature. "Look at me."

Philip reluctantly pulled down the blanket. Standing before him was a priest, the same priest that was in his dreams, only he was so much older. He was dressed in a blue robe with a large hood. His face was noble, like that of a knight, a king, a lion.

"Soon, Mr. Parker, you shall have your answers." He spoke in a loud clear voice.

Philip moved closer, still trembling, "Who are you?"

"Seek he who shares your dreams. He will help you."

"Who is it?" Philip asked timidly.

"The young lad, seek the young lad," with that, the creature turned and headed back to the wall. "Together, you can kill it. Seek the boy."

The creature walked back into the wall, back into a shadow, and flying across the room, was gone.

Jimmy heard a voice in the night, a soft wonderful voice. At first, he thought it was a thought deep in his mind, but it was so clear, so soft.

"Jimmy, you are a man, stop being such a fool."

Jimmy lay half frightened to death, but that voice, so kind and caring.

"They say you are slow. They lie. Momma is being mean to you. She wants you to be slow so that she can control you. She hates you, Jimmy. She has always hated you."

"No," said Jimmy into the darkness.

"Wouldn't it be nice if she were gone, Jimmy? Do as I say and you will be happier than you ever dreamed, I promise you, just let me in."

"In where?"

"Inside of you Jimmy, I'm the only one who cares."

"I know who you are, you're the devil, I've heard of you."

"I am what you want me to be Jimmy, but most of all I am your friend. I have the power to make you smart, Jimmy. Just let me in."

"No!"

"You'll never have to look for cans again, Jimmy."

"You'll never have to touch another man for money."

"Stop, you're hurting my head"

"But I want to be your friend, I see you Jimmy, I have always seen you."

"You want to be my friend?"

"Yes Jimmy, your friend."

"You can make me smart?"

"Yes Jimmy, I will fill all your dreams."

"Oh please, just go away, I don't want you here."

Suddenly the voice changed, less kind, less caring, more forceful: "Alright, I'll go for now, but think about it, Jimmy. I can make you a real man, not the sick twisted wimp you are now." And the words stopped.

Jimmy lay back on his bed scared and confused. Happy, smart, friend, wimp, all these words repeated in his head.

Ken Jones was getting ready for bed. Sporting his striped cotton pajamas and slippers, he made his way to the kitchen to get his coffeepot ready for the morning, or in reality, the afternoon. For those who own a bar, four in the morning was night-time and noon was morning. Through the years, he had gotten used to the schedule and it would have seemed unnatural to live as others did.

His apartment above the bar was quaint, a single bedroom, a small living room area, an open kitchen/dining room and bath. He had lived contentedly there for years. He once owned a house on Maple, but when his wife passed, he moved into the apartment above the bar and had remained there. As modest as the space was, it did not compete with its less than meager furnishings. His living room resembled a patio with a wicker couch and matching chair. An ancient RCA was placed squarely on a wooden beer barrel he had bought from the Schlitz Brewing Company in Detroit when they were in their heyday. In his bedroom, there was a single bed, no headboard, and a stand up dresser. His kitchen table was in reality a card table with a tablecloth draped over the top.

Jones' Bar made good money, but at his age, he did not feel a need for the better things in life. If he was going to blow his dough, it would be better spent at the horse track in Jackson. Man, he loved to watch those sulkies trot. His next favorite past time was betting on football, even though he had lost his ass through the years on the Lions, the Wolverines had put some serious jack in his pocket.

After setting up the coffeepot he grabbed Tigger, the best friend he ever had, at least that is what he told everyone, and started lugging her out the doorway and down the steps to the exterior door. She was in heat and would drive him nuts if he didn't put her out. Cats like Tigger were a bitch when they wanted out and couldn't get there. Down the steps he trotted. As he opened the downstairs door the cat started to squirm; without warning she started digging deep into his arms with her claws. She always liked getting out, but this was a little much, even for her. He gently tossed her outside and shut the door. Halfway back up the steps, he heard the door reopen. What the hell, maybe he'd forgotten to shut it all the way and the wind caught it; this would not have been the first time he had done that.

He never got the chance to turn, as something grabbed his leg and gave a hard, swift pull. Down he went, his hands clutching for anything they could hold on to. Before he had even hit the steps, it was on him, a blurred white apparition in the dark. He felt his pajama top being ripped from his chest then a sharp agonizing pain in his gut. Instinctively, Ken brought down his elbow hard and it connected with the things skull, it collapsed to one side and lay lifeless, blood smeared across it repugnant face. Ken reached down and felt a gaping hole in his midsection. The bastard had bitten him, had taken a huge fucking bit right out of him. The pile of shit was still lying on top of him so he kicked as hard as he could with both legs and it went air borne for a moment before tumbling down the rest of the steps. There it lay, motionless. Ken tried to get up, he could feel the blood rushing from his body. He had to do something, and he had to do it quickly. As he forced himself to his hands and knees, dizziness engulfed him and he had to lay back down. So, this is what it's like to die, he thought. After a moment, the dizziness began to subside and momentarily, his mind began to clear. He was not going to bleed to death in his own home. Slowly, he got back up, with one hand holding his stomach, he started crawling inch by endless inch up the stairs. Each movement was purposeful, as each motion was a new experience in torcher. After an eternity, he rounded the corner at the top of the stairs and crept through the open door.

I'm not going to let this baster kill me, he told himself. On the end table near the couch was the phone, just a few more feet now. Once again sharp pains radiated from his gut, and he went down once again. He could feel his own innards trying to flop out onto the open floor. Exhausted, his body spent, just one good reach, one long stretch and he would be there. Ken paused, he knew his time was short but he had to rest, he had to build up what strength was left. He wondered if he would be able to dial, let alone speak to anyone. But he also knew he had to try. His very life depended on it. Lying on the floor, he heard nothing but his own breath, labored and short. Not a sound did he hear from the stairway. After what seemed an endlessness amount of time, he mustered all that he had and flung himself at the phone, but he was stopped inches from his own salvation.

Through the doorway, a white claw had snuck up from behind. In a flash it clinched Ken's foot and jerked so hard it launched him in the air and slammed him into the doorway, then it slowly dragged him back down into the darkened stairway as Ken screamed and screamed.

It was five in the morning when Martha and Jake returned home. Mrs. Cartwright's story had left Martha shaken and for the first time ever, she made sure the house was locked up before meeting Jake in the kitchen.

"Well," said Jake as she entered. "What do you think?"

"I don't know what to think," she answered. She walked over and put on water for coffee, she knew she would not get any sleep that night, after all that had occurred. That poor girl, how could this have happened? And right next door, in the house of a good friend?

"Mrs. Cartwright seems to think that she was pushed out that window doesn't she?" asked Jake.

"Yes, there was obviously someone in her apartment from the sounds of things."

"I just can't believe something like this is taking place in Parksville," said Jake, as he sat down at the table. He was shaking his head in disbelief.

"I am worried about Brandy, you should have heard her go on and on about that black bird being in the house. It's as if she's trying to put the blame on herself by applying some old wives' tale. Poor old soul. I wish I could have talked her into coming over, or at least letting me stay with her."

"She is a brave one, that's for sure."

"You know what she told me when I asked her to spend the night?"

"No, what?"

"She said that the devil himself could not drive her out of her own house. You know, I think she meant it."

"What are we going to tell Franky?" asked Jake.

"The truth, I guess."

"He will be devastated. Oh Aunt Martha, I just feel so sorry for him. I know he really cared for this girl." Just then, the kettle began to whistle.

Martha got up, "Would you like a cup?"

"Sure, I'm not going to get any sleep tonight, anyway. Not after all of this."

"How is your mom doing? God I miss her." Martha said as she poured hot water into the cups of instant coffee. She was trying to change the subject, obviously ready to talk about anything else at this point. The night had been rough on both of them, and she didn't even want to think about what poor Brandy must be going through.

"Good I guess, you know her, she acts like she has never had a bad day in her life."

Martha handed Jake his cup and sat down looking at him with a caring smile. "That is what I miss most about her. She was always able to make a sunny day out of a winter storm."

"Did she tell you about the cancer?" Jake asking in a tone that showed he already knew the answer.

"Yes, I know, of course she didn't tell me I had to hear it from your Aunt Heather. Your mom would never say a word."

"She has to have both her breast removed, she said they were looking at July for the surgery. It was her choice, she could have had the treatment, but she doesn't want to take any chances. I am going to be there of course, and help her as much as I can."

"You're a good boy Jake, but I think she is going to need more than just you. I am calling her in the morning and letting her know I am coming up in July and taking care of her until she is on her feet. I have a lot of vacation time and I do not know how better to use it."

"You know she'll tell you not to bother" Jake grinned.

"Of course she will, but you know that won't stop me."

"I know"

"I want to thank you for what you did for Franky. He needed you in his life again."

"I never left; he just wouldn't let me in"

"That's because he is so much like your father."

"My father, how?"

"Pig headed. I loved your Dad more than anyone, but he was pig headed. Stubborn as the day is long."

Jake was taken aback. He had never heard anyone talk about his father this way. He started to chuckle. "Was he really?"

"Yes, Franky may look like his father, but there is so much of your father in him that there are times I forget which one I'm talking too. I remember one time your father did not say a word to me for almost a month, all because I caught him comparing the size of his pecker with Bill Brice from down the street."

Jake broke out with laughter, "Pecker?"

"Oh please, neither one of them even had anything to look at for God's sake, they were eleven years old. Man he was pissed when he saw me standing there, me with my mouth wide open."

Jake lost it, maybe it was the lack of sleep, maybe it was dealing with the shock of a dead girl across the road, but he could not stop laughing.

Martha joined in with a few giggles of her own. "Anyway, not a word for a month."

Jake slowly regained his composure, "Aunt Martha, was my Dad a good man."

"Your Dad was the best, we were ever so close. I was so happy that he and Frank got along so well. The two men I loved most in the world became the very best of friends, you just cannot ask for more than that." She reached over and put her hand on Jake's, and smiled. "Jake honey, I know you were very small when your Daddy died. I know you loved him with all your heart, and I know it about killed you when he went away. But truly, the closest you'll ever get to know him as a man, the way that Frank new him, is by getting to know that young man up there in bed. He is just like him."

Philip did not get out of bed until noon. He could not believe he had slept so long. Last night had been a large drain on his mind and apparently his body. He felt achy all over, and moved at a snail's pace throughout the house. When he finally made his way into the living room, he switched on the TV, and there was Susan's face. "Another murder took place late last night in the small town of Parksville. Details on your nightly news . . ."

Philip quickly turned off the set.

"Seek the boy."

What boy? How in the hell was he supposed to look for someone when he didn't even know who or where they were.

"You can kill him."

Him, that part Philip did know. Fritz, the creature from the field. Philip had witnessed his art of dining on human flesh. In an odd way, he felt some comfort in the knowledge that his foe was not a mystery, not totally. He knew what he looked like, and he could never forget those eyes. Philip made up his mind right then. First, he would keep his promise to Kip: go and see this Sam guy. Then he would work on finding this boy. The old manor may hold some answers. Maybe he would go there as well, but if he did, he would have to go before dark. Something about that place frightened the shit out of him. If this Fritz creature did happen to be around, he would not be strong enough to kill him alone.

"Seek the boy."

Fuck, I wish this whole thing would never have happened. Philip knew the stakes were now higher than he ever imagined, for the salvation of those who had died at Fritz's hands were now his cross to bear.

He had taken his time getting ready then, on the spur of the moment, decided to stop and get a dozen roses for Martha. Martha's face had lit up when she saw him walking through the door with the bouquet clinched tightly in his hands. After a quick lunch at the local Burger King, Philip dropped her off back at her office and headed to the hospital.

It was three by the time he arrived at Sam's office. Though he had been to the hospital a hundred times, he still got lost every time he went there. This time was no exception, compounded by the fact that he had never been to Sam's office, or anywhere near the morgue. Philip wandered endlessly reading directional signs until he was finally saved by a young male nurse who happened to be going in that direction.

Sam, who had been expecting Philip, was more than happy at his arrival. He seemed more than willing to help Philip with whatever he needed, as if it were a relief to share the burden of concealment.

"Kip told me I could trust you," said Sam in his soft voice. "Bibens still has not caught wind that he is down here. After all, he has nothing to do with the rest of the killings, not yet anyway. If he presses me, I will have to give him my report, I doubt however, he would believe it. So far, the only ones who know what is going on here is Kip and me."

Philip liked Sam right off the bat. He could tell by the man's eyes that he was sincere and his loyalty to Kip was obvious. Anyone who would go as far as letting this information go to a complete stranger while holding it from a Federal Agent was loyal to a fault.

Philip had never seen the inside of a morgue, but when he entered, it looked just like he had imagined. On one wall was row after row of doors, each stacked upon one another, here now lay the bodies of those killed by Fritz. The same people who haunted his dreams were just out of sight.

"He is back here," said Sam pointing to a door on the opposite wall.

Philip assumed this was the room where they do the autopsies. There were two metal tables and glass cupboards filled with any number of medical instruments. On the far table lay a figure covered with a white sheet.

"Has Kip given you any background on this case?" asked Sam.

"Nothing on the boy."

"Well, it seemed pretty open and shut. The boy's father beat him and his brother and it was assumed that the boy died of such wounds. With all that has happened lately, no one has pressed me to prove it. Mr. Cooper is still laid up in the hospital anyway. From what they say, it may be another three weeks."

"Laid up? Why?"

"Well, they said he was attacked by a bird. Can you believe it? Kip said it was the damnedest thing he'd ever seen."

"Cooper. This wouldn't be Josh Cooper's boy would it?"

"Yeah, that's it. Josh Cooper."

"I went to school with him. He was an asshole then, too."

Sam peeled back the sheet and there lay Scotty Cooper, just as they had found him. "He looks like he's sleeping. No life signs what so ever, no death signs either. No brain activity, no pulse, and no breath, yet no rigor mortis and no discoloring."

Philip lifted the boys arm. It was perfectly limp, but there were no signs of death. Philip remembered when he was small and his father had passed away. He was there in the house when it happened. He remembered hugging his father one last time before they took him away. He felt different. He felt empty, dead. This, he did not feel from the boy.

"I just don't know what to think," said Sam shaking his head.

"It's like he is in suspended animation," said Philip.

"That's it. That's it exactly. I have been thinking of some way of phrasing it, but I think you hit it right on the button. Too bad I can't write that in my report."

"This whole thing is so beyond belief," Philip answered in agreement waiting to see Sam's response.

"Look Philip, I do not know how much you already know, or how you got involved in all this, all I know is that Kip said you could be trusted and that you would report everything to him, but do you know those other people, the ones who were killed in Parksville? They were eaten alive."

"I know, I was there when they found the Gibsons."

"Well, did you know the wounds are changing?" asked Sam.

Now, this was something new, Sam now had his undivided attention.

"The bite radius has remained the same, but the teeth marks are getting duller. You see the first girl looked like she was the victim of a shark bite. That is how razor-sharp the teeth marks were.

While the change is not dramatic, they are there all the same. The last couple, the Gibsons, the teeth marks were more . . . well, human. You see this thing, whatever it is . . ."

Philip had a good idea but didn't let on.

". . . is changing, evolving as it were. Either that, or every person was killed by a different person, who just happens to have the exact same sized mouth."

"Does Kip know this?"

"Not yet, last time I went to see him, they watched me like a hawk. They think I know more than I'm letting on, and they are right. The only problem is that they would not believe me if I told them. This whole case is unnatural. Something evil is going on here. You try telling Bibens there is a monster loose in Parksville."

"Well, I am picking Kip up tomorrow, so I guess I can fill him in then. At least I know he will believe me. Anything else?" Philip asked giving him a sympathetic glance.

"No, I guess that's everything," said Sam. As he covered the boy with the sheet he added, "I told them that you were a relative who would be willing to pay for the funeral. I only hope he doesn't need one."

On his way home, Philip drove through downtown. At this point, his mind was a total blank, it seems the mind can only handle so much before it needs a break. His radio was blaring an old tune by the band War and the sun shining through his window made him feel warm and safe. The city was alive with activity, something one seldom sees in Jackson these days, and somehow life seemed uncommonly normal. That is, until he came upon the county jail.

The entire street was filled with activity. Police car after police car filed into the parking lot with any number of reporters on their heels. Philip parked his car along the road and got out. Quickly, he ran down the street just in time to see a man being hauled out of the first car with his face hidden behind his own coat. In a flash, he was surrounded by a crowd of people, shouting questions and flashing their cameras. Without thinking, Philip threw himself into the fray. Swimming with the sea of endless bodies, Philip pushed his way toward the front in order to get a glimpse of the man being dragged along.

By the time he got up to where he could see, they had the man inside and the door was shut tight behind them. "Who was that?" he asked a young woman struggling with a large video camera. "That, my friend, is the Parksville slasher. Cops got him just a little while ago."

"Oh my God" said Philip in response. Philip wanted to believe all of this, if he had to he would force himself to deny all he knew was true and accept the outcome. They got him. Monster or man, he was now behind bars.

Philip turned and started back toward his car. Just then, he saw Franky Lake's head bobbing along the crowd. Franky seemed to see him at the same moment and ran off in the other direction. Philip watched him as he made his way across the street and jumped into Jake's van. In a flash he was gone.

"What in the world?" Philip said aloud. Suddenly, Philip felt a light tug on his shoulder. Turning around he saw Sam.

"Look, right after you left I got word to report here. It seems they found another body and the guy who's behind all of this. I cannot tell you anymore because I don't know anymore. Tell Kip I will give word." Sam turned and headed back into the crowd.

It was true. They caught the bastard. A mountain of nerves seemed to slide from his body. It was over, thank God, it was over. Maybe this guy was the Fritz from his dreams, maybe he was just going crazy, but it was over.

A cheer went out in Martha's office as the news of the Parksville Slasher's arrest came over the radio. Martha was working with a customer at the time, but even she could not help giving out a small "YES." Earlier in the day, she had heard the report about Sue Barkley's death. They stated that she probably had been the victim of a failed robbery attempt. However, Martha still felt that whoever had been doing all those killings was behind this.

It was hard to believe that one murderer could be loose in Parksville. Let alone two.

Martha turned to the customer sitting there and said, "Well, Father McMurry, it looks like your loan for the school has come through. St. Timothy's is going to get its new pool after all."

Philip could hardly wait to talk to Kip. After leaving the scene at the jailhouse, Philip treated himself to a nice dinner and a restful stroll through downtown. It was hard to believe it was all over. Maybe a little too hard. Still, Philip would not give into pessimism.

As he walked throughout the hospital to Kip's room, Philip noticed no police officers or FBI men anywhere around. Bibens must have given up his watch over Kip now that the case had been solved. As he entered the room with a gleam in his eyes, Kip, who was sitting up in a chair near the window, quickly motioned for him to close the door behind him.

"That idiot Bibens is so fucking far off the mark, that he needs a surgeon to pull his head out of his ass," Kip huffed.

Obviously, word had reached him.

"Have a seat, Phil. So did you hear about the Parksville Slasher?" he said mockingly.

"Yeah, I was down to the jail when they brought him in." Philip made his way to the corner of Kip's bed and sat down facing him. Even though he had tried to force himself into believing, he could not. Now he was sure there would never be that chance.

"Officer Cowan, you know her from the Gibson's house," started Kip.

"Yes, I remember."

"Well, it seems she was driving into Parksville when she passed Jimmy Martinez. You know, the guy who used to walk around Parksville collecting cans and bottles off the side of the road."

"You mean Jerky Jimmy." said Philip. He never could stand that guy. He gave him the creeps. He was always so freaky, so dirty.

"Yeah, that's the one. Anyway, Cowan stopped him to ask where he was going. Well, it seems that he came right out and told her that he had been doing the killings in Parksville, the devil told him to. At first, Cowan thought that he was crazy, then this Jimmy guy tells her that he has something to show her. He got into her car and together they rode to his mother's house on Michigan Ave. You know that big scary place just before town that sits way back on that hill."

"Yeah, I know the place."

"Well it seems that Jimmy really did have something to show Cowan. When Cowan got to the house, Jimmy's mother was dead on the floor of her living room. It seems that little Jimmy had gutted her with a small garden tool. I guess the scene looked a lot like something our killer would leave behind. What do you think?"

"I think Jimmy probably did kill his mother. The bastard always did give me the heebie-geebies, but there is no way he could have brought down Big Bill, no way, not that skinny little fuck."

"You got it. But it gets better. Cowan calls in the report. She has in custody a man claiming to be the Parksville Slasher, (his term) and that she found a body that he in fact led her to which matches those previously found. She is told to hold the suspect on the scene until Bibens can get there. God only knows how the press got a hold of it, but Cowan said they beat Bibens to the scene. Anyway, while she waited with this asshole in the back seat of her car, she asked him again if he committed the murders in Parksville. He stated the devil told him to. She then asked if he had killed his mother. He said 'yes, he had to, the devil told him to.' 'Why are you admitting to all of this,' she asked. 'Because the devil told me to,' he says. And then he says, 'the devil has such beautiful blue eyes, did you know that?'"

Kip immediately noticed the look in Philip's eyes. "Look Phil, we all desire an end to this, but whoever is behind this is not stupid, they know what they are doing. Now, first I want you to tell me what Sam said about the boy, then I want you to come clean with whatever it is you know or think you know about this case, regardless of how stupid it may sound when you do. Then, when you are done, there are a few things I can tell you. You see, a few days of rest, and a little less drugs have helped me remember everything that happened at the old manor."

Philip didn't even hesitate; he looked into Kip's eyes and realized that he was right. When he started talking, he could not stop. He told all that Sam had said, he told him about his dreams, he told him everything that he could possibly remember starting with the day it all started. All the time he talked Kip listened without a word.

When Philip was done Kip began. It was dark by the time they were finally done and they both had come to one conclusion, the war would begin on the next day.

The drive home was long and silent for Philip. He left off the radio because he needed to think. As he came up to his house, he saw Jake's van parked along the street. As he rounded the corner into his drive, he spotted Franky Lake sitting on his porch swing.

"Hi, Mr. Parker," said Franky as Philip made his way up the front steps. Franky's head was hung down between his shoulders and he did not bother to look up.

Philip could tell at once that the boy was distraught. "What's wrong, Franky?" Philip asked sympathetically.

"Well, I know you are not going to believe me when I tell you this, but damn, I just have to tell someone before I go crazy." Finally, he looked up at Philip with confusion in his eyes. "You see, I've been having these dreams."

WEDNESDAY

"Well Captain Gillmore, it looks like you get to go home today," said Dr. Rose as he entered the room. "You do want to go home don't you?"

Kip waited until the doctor looked up from his chart then gave him a nod of his head.

"Look Captain, I know that you want out of here, but I am going to tell you to take it easy, and I mean it. It is going to take time to heal, so don't rush it. Now, I will be seeing you a week from Tuesday, I have already made your appointment."

All the time the doctor spoke, Kip was looking out of the window at the beautiful sunlight. Outside he could see a great oak, with a large black bird singing his morning song.

"Now, is there someone you want us to call to take you home?"

"No I have someone coming, but could you let him know I am ready?"

"Sure, I'll have the nurse call"

Philip had just fallen back to sleep when the phone rang. "Hello, Mr. Parker."

"Yes, this is Parker, can I help you?"

"Yes this is Nurse Johnson at Jackson Memorial Hospital. I'm calling on behalf of a Mr. Kip Gillmore. He is being released today, and he wondered if you would be kind enough to pick him up."

"Sure, I already had plans to do so."

"Fine, he will be ready within the hour."

"Well thank you, good-bye."

"Good-bye sir."

As Philip hung up the phone, he could not help but think that getting out was going to be the best thing for Gillmore. The time of doubt was over, his little talk with Franky had confirmed that. The boy, of course, Philip should have known all along that Franky was in fact the one sharing his dreams. Philip had no idea of what was going to happen that day, but one thing he was sure of, someone may not be around to tell the tale.

As soon as Franky opened his eyes, he jumped out of bed and started getting ready. As he passed the open door of his bedroom, he could hear conversation coming from downstairs. He wondered if he was the topic and quietly made his way down the hallway and stood at the top of the stairs trying to pick up on the conversation.

"What are you going to do this morning, Jake?"

"I really haven't given it much thought, why?"

"I think it would be nice if you ran into Jackson and got some flowers for Franky to send to her folks."

They were talking about Sue. How odd that situation had been last night when she had confronted him with it.

"While I'm in town, I think I will get something for Mrs. Cartwright, too," came Jake's voice again.

"I think that would be real nice of you, after all she has been through. I'm sure she would appreciate it."

"Have you heard anything new?"

"The police say that she got into a fight with a robber who threw her out of the window".

"Is that what you think really happened?"

"With everything that has been going on in this town in the past few weeks, I don't know what to believe."

"Well, I'm just glad they caught that one nut."

Franky laughed in spite of himself, if you only knew, he thought.

"The first girl he ever liked, you know I was really starting to wonder what his chances were of ever finding one."

"Well, his chances are a lot better now."

"No kidding, that look of his was pretty pathetic."

"Well, I might as well get going," said Jake.

Franky could hear the chair slide across the floor as Jake got up. He did not know what to do. He did not feel up to facing either one of them, there was no way he could keep the secret he held inside without giving something away. He made up his mind and went bolting down the stairs past Jake who had just come out of the kitchen.

"Franky," yelled Jake, but it was too late. Franky had already opened the door and walked outside without any sign of recognition.

Martha came running out of the kitchen. "Do you think he heard us?"

"I don't know, you want me to go after him?"

"No, if he did hear us, he probably would rather be alone," said Martha, "how stupid could I be?"

"Now Aunt Martha, we do not know if he heard us or not, besides, how were we to know he was listening."

"I know, I just feel so bad for him."

"I'm sure he will be all right."

"I know, but to hear us talking about him like that," Martha said shaking her head.

Franky walked into the bright morning sunlight. It had already gotten warm and the morning dew sparkled on the grass. A million thoughts were going through his head as he tried to recall all that he and Professor Parker had talked about. In regards to their dreams, they had been the exact same, even with the arrivals of Susan. That part had almost brought both of them to tears. The fact that they had shared these experiences together had somehow formed a bond that is hard to explain, as if they were always meant to be partners in this struggle against the forces of evil. It seems so clear to him now, the stranger in the woods, the presence forever hovering in the darkness of his sub-conscience. Franky was curious if this feeling of closeness that they had shared the night before would be as strong in the light of day. Was their bond held only by fear that the night enhanced? This he would soon find out.

As he made his way up the steps of Professor Parker's front porch, Franky had the strangest feeling that his life was never going to be the same. Lightly, he tapped on the front door.

"Come on in Franky," said Philip.

Franky opened the door. He offered a smile and got one in return. Philip led him into the kitchen and there offered him a cup of coffee and a bite to eat. Franky agreed only to the coffee, he did not feel much like eating. Philip shared that same feeling, and he too settled for just coffee. The two men sat staring at each other, it was obvious they were looking for something to say.

"Well, what do we do now?" Franky said at last.

"Now you come with me to town. We have to pick up a friend of mine at the hospital." answered Philip. "He is the only one to see the bastard and still be alive to talk about it."

"He has seen Fritz? Where?"

"In the old manor."

"Where is he now? Do you think he is still there?"

"I don't know. Right now, we need to go into Jackson. You want me to give your mom a call?"

"No, not really," said Franky. "I had a hell of a time actually talking to her about Sue. It's hard when you know something but can't tell anyone."

"Sue was an exceptional girl," said Philip. "Well, we must be going, are you ready?"

"As ready as I'll ever be."

"Good, on the way I will fill you in on what else I have learned."

In darkest corner of the manor's rat infested attic, a dark figure moved silently about. It sat next to an open porthole window, which let just enough light shine through to make out the features of a man. From the outside came a high-pitched squawk then suddenly the room was alive with the sound of wings in flight.

"Come to me, my pet," came a voice that sounded more like the hiss of a snake than that of a human. "Come here, you black little bassstard and greet your masssster."

The black bird lit upon the shapeless shoulder, again squawking loud and full.

"Yesss, you have done well my pet, but now I need you for sssomething elssse. Forget that fool who invaded my home for now. He ssshall sssee me again in due time, I promissse you but for now, I want information. Thossse foolsss I have ssspoken of are getting clossser to the truth all the time. I can feel it. I know not what powers they consssseal, but there mussst be sssome reassson for that Priessst to have chosssen them. I could sssee into their pitiful little dreamsss sssoo easssily, if only I had the power to have followed them on their little way back home, what a nissse sssurprissse I could have given them."

The large black bird now flew to the other side of the room.

"Oh my poor little pet, jussst think, when I am done, you ssshall be your own pitiful little ssself again. You would like that, wouldn't you? But for now you are mine."

The bird let out another squawk.

A moan escaped the dark figure, "the pain." He laid a large claw-like hand upon his abdomen, "how many more before I am whole and get the powersss promisssed to me. I would be clossse if it wasssn't for that bitch getting away, the pain, I ssshall have to have another tonight or I doubt I can bare it. The one lassst night isss not taking the pain from me. If I were ssstill in my own time, I would have had enough by now, but who can figure out thessse beguiling timesss when a man travelsss by machine rather than horssse. Their homesss and ssstreetsss forever aglow. If not for you my pet, I would be at a total losss. For you are my earsss, my eyessss."

The bird gave no response.

"If not for you, I could never have found that mindlesss fool. He wasss so easssy to control. The way he took to killing wasss a sssight. Now he will take all the blame, the proof of hisss killingsss, in hisss own two little handsss, and he will never be able to sssay anything different, will he?"

Again, there was no response from the bird. He simply stared back with cold, black eyes.

"Now, my friend, I call upon you again. Find me a way to draw the two sssstrangers to me. I may not have the time I thought to wait. All of my powersss have yet to come to me, ssso I mussst fassse them here, on my own termsss and in my own home. Now take to the air, my pet. Find me what I need. Go, go!"

Suddenly, the room again became animated with the sound of fluttering wings, then all became deathly still as the creature bent his head to sleep.

Franky stared aimlessly out the window as Philip talked. The MG was getting a rattle somewhere in the rear. Needs new shocks, thought Franky. The sun was still shining high in the eastern sky. Philip was forced to transfer his visor to block it from blinding him from the oncoming traffic. The winters in this state were long and hard but the springs were unpredictable. It had been rather pleasant this year, but on any given day, winter could return to say its goodbyes. Regardless, spring always brought new life. How ironic thought Franky, that all of this would start this time of year.

He tried to block the whole thing out of his mind and focus on what Philip was talking about. He had no idea that he had become so involved to have actually gone into a house where deceased people lay on their beds, torn apart. It was becoming very overwhelming for him.

When Philip was done talking, he looked over at Franky, who had yet to utter a word. He had asked no questions and offered no input but only sat there, watching out of the passenger window. Philip could comprehend why. All of this was tough to face. He knew in his own time he would respond. For now, maybe the best thing was simply to enjoy this delightful morning. He thought of how nice it would be going places this summer with Martha, the beach, parks, maybe a concert at Pine Knob. The winters may be hell here, but the summers were hard to beat and at Pine Knob one could enjoy a concert the way they were meant to be, out in the open under a vibrant blue sky, with a cold beer in hand, sitting on a blanket, just the two of them. Without cause, his thoughts briefly went to Sue and how she had told him that she loved him. He wondered if it would have made a difference to him. One thing was true, she had waited too long to say it. He made up his mind right then, that the next time he saw Martha, he would tell her he treasured her. Who knows, the next time may be the last. Though they had dated only a few times, he knew in his heart that she was everything that he had yearned for.

He looked over to Franky, who offered a smile then turned back to the window. Philip had just noticed the change in the boy, his hair was short and his gear was far from what he typically had seen the boy wearing. Franky looked much older, more mature. He wondered if this was the work of Martha, or if his cousin had brought him into the twentieth century, whatever the reason, it was a marked improvement.

"You might think I am crazy, but with all that has been going on, I just now noticed that you got your hair cut," said Philip. "It really looks nice on you."

"Thank you," said Franky. "I had it cut at the shop in town."

"It's a lot different than it used to be."

"That's what I was aiming for," reasoned Franky with a grin. "I also picked up some new clothes and things. Jake picked out most of them actually, I have such lousy taste."

"Well, that was pretty nice of him."

"Yeah, I guess so, but the nicest thing was that he paid for them." They both began to laugh. It felt good to laugh again.

"My mom really digs you, you know."

"Really," said Philip a little blushed, "what makes you say that?"

"I can tell."

"Well I like her too." He still felt uneasy talking to Franky about her, as if he were afraid of his disapproval. It was as though he was going to say any minute, *stay away from my mother, you loser.*

"Well, I think it is great," said Franky. "Mom needs someone to make her happy."

"That will be an easier job after this is all over."

The feeling of gloom that had hovered over the car returned and the two sat in silence for a moment.

"Who knows," ventured Franky at last, "maybe the two of you will get married."

Philip's eyes widened and a small gasp escaped his lips.

"Maybe I will start calling you Daddy".

Philip looked at Franky with shock upon his face.

Franky at once broke out in laughter.

Through a suppressed grin, Philip said, "I will settle for Philip if you don't mind."

"Philip, I don't know if I could get used to that, but I guess it would be better than introducing you as my mother and Professor Parker."

"Well let's not get carried away just yet, there, Mr. Lake."

"Do I get to be the best man?" asked Franky, "Do I, huh?"

"Shit, you will be lucky to be invited."

"Seriously," said Franky, "if you ever did marry mother, I would be very happy."

"Thank you, that is a very nice thing to say."

"Then I can make both of your lives a living hell."

Philip's grin now turned into laughter, he was quickly joined by Franky.

Green pastures finally gave way to city streets and before long, they were parked in front of Jackson's only thriving hospital. It was one of the biggest in the state, but with all the modernization the personal charm of the old hospital that once stood there, was gone. The two were still snickering and joking as they made their way inside. As they stepped into the new lobby, the nurse at the front desk took notice of them, "can I help you?"

"Yes," said Philip. "We are here to pick up a Mr. Gillmore."

"Do you have a room number?"

"Yes, Room 359," said Philip. As he spoke, he noticed the way in which the cute young nurse was giving Franky the eye. Franky seemed not to notice.

"Well go right on up then," she said grinning ear to ear in Franky's direction, "and have a nice day."

Franky gave no response.

"You too," said Philip, and with that he turned toward the elevator. That boy still has a lot to learn, he thought.

When arriving in Kip's room, Philip was surprised to find him still not dressed. "I thought you would be ready by now."

Kip at once gave a questioning look at Franky.

"Oh, this is Franky Lake, a dear friend of mine."

Franky was taken by surprise at the introduction.

"Franky, this is Captain Gillmore of the JPD."

"Pleased to meet you," said Franky and offered his hand.

Gillmore reached out and shook it. Lake, he thought. He had heard that name before but couldn't place it.

"So what's going on, why the delay?" asked Philip.

"They never told me they cut my clothes off me, I have nothing to put on. I tried to call you back this morning but you must have been on your way."

Philip gave his little grin, "you mean you have nothing at all to wear home?"

"No, nothing, I was wondering if you wouldn't mind . . ."

"You're really getting to be a pain in the ass, you know that don't you."

"What are friends for?" answered Kip.

"Give me your keys and I will get something from your apartment."

"They're in that drawer over there," said Kip. Again, he looked over at Franky who was standing near the door.

"I will explain everything once we get you home."

It took a total of two and a half hours for Philip and Franky to go to Kip's apartment, bring him an outfit to wear home, for him to get dressed, for transportation to arrive to take him downstairs and for them to return to his apartment. The minute they entered Kip's modest two-bedroom apartment, Philip began telling Kip about how he and Franky had shared the same dreams. Philip thought Franky might be a little wary about talking about all of this to a stranger, let alone the captain of the local police department, but he joined right in and filled in the gaps when he felt Philip had left out significant information.

As for Kip, he sat and listened to every word not showing any signs of disbelief. A few times, he had wanted to ask questions, but thought better of it.

When Philip had finished, he turned to Kip: "remember when I told you that the priest in my dreams told me to seek the boy? Well, it seems he sought me out instead."

Like Franky, Kip reached for his own security blanket that was no longer there. For Franky, it was his long red hair, for Kip it was his mustache that had been shaved off to stitch a small cut on his upper lip. It was his practice to twist it when confronted with a difficult question or problem, but now the best he could do was run his hand along the bare spot. "Well, that is some story. When I asked you to look into this case, who would have believed it."

"Look, I know it's all hard to believe."

"Oh get real, Philip! After what I told you last night, you think I'm not going to believe this, you forget, I saw that bastard, it wasn't human, it was evil, pure evil. If this young man was sent to help, all I can say is Thank God."

A look of relief came over Franky's face knowing that he was being accepted.

The look on Philip's face was the opposite. Not that he did not want Franky, or Kip for that matter, to help him; he just wondered if everyone who took part in this realized they may not live to see it through.

Kip, being the cop he was, stated, "Look, we have to start going through those dreams with a fine-tooth comb. I can't believe this priest of yours would go through all of this trouble without telling you how to kill it."

Just then, the phone began to ring. Kip reached over the side of his lazy boy and answered it off the large end table.

"Yes, I see." He spoke into the phone. After a moment, he added. "Thanks Cowan, you're a good cop." Then he hung it back up. "Well, it seems our friend has been busy. They found Jimmy Martinez this morning. It seems he found some extra floor stripper laying around and swigged it with his morning coffee. When they found him, he was sitting in his cell with a note clutched in his hand that said something like, *I am sorry for what I have done and if you need further proof that I did it check out the bar in Parksville.* They did and found Kenny lain out like a Sweden House Buffet. They sent the body down to Sam's office but as far as Bibens is concerned the case is over."

"Why don't you call Sam and see what he found out?" asked Philip.

Kip shook his head and picked up the phone once more. He was about to hang up when Sam answered.

Again, Franky and Philip were forced to wait until he had finished. When once again he hung up the phone, he turned to the two waiting. "Sam says the time of death was the same as Mrs. Martinez. That means there is no way that Jimmy could have done it. You can't kill two people on opposite sides of town at the same time."

"Has Sam told Bibens this?" asked Philip.

"Not yet, he hasn't been able to confirm it yet, but he will, Sam is good at what he does. Knowing Sam he will stall him as long as he can," answered Kip.

"That Sam seems to be a good guy," responded Philip.

"The best," said Kip. "Now you must try and remember everything that priest said or did in your dream. If we are going after this bastard, something tells me we are going to get one chance, and one chance only. We cannot afford to fuck it up. He may not know a lot about modern forensics, but he was smart enough to get to Jimmy last night."

"Kip is right, we have to do this right away," said Philip. "Now, let's see. The priest was having the hooded ones thrown into a fire, remember?" he said to Franky.

"Yeah, he was just kneeling there praying, and the next thing you know, they would bring out another one and whomp, there they went in a flash."

"And all the time he was praying, he never looked up once," added Philip.

Kip looked puzzled for a moment then looked up. "What was the prayer?"

"I don't recall, it was in Latin, I think," answered Philip.

"We need a Holy man then to pray while he burns," said Kip.

"He was holding a large crucifix, a gold one, in his hands," added Franky.

"Great," said Philip, he slunk down onto the couch, "all we have to do is find a priest, as crazy as we are, packing a loaded cross."

With this Kip smiled. "I think I have just the man for the job."

Martha Lake was feeling more than a little concerned. She had arrived home early from work, telling everyone she was going to a Greater Jackson Area Business meeting, to find that Franky had never returned home that day. She looked up at the clock; it was nearing the two o'clock hour and still no word. She at once sent Jake out to look, but he had yet to check in. Maybe she shouldn't have let him go like that. Maybe she should have sat him down and . . . "and what?" she said out loud.

Suddenly, she heard a loud screech from Franky's room. She jumped at the sound. "What the hell was that?" she whispered to herself. Standing up from the kitchen table, she turned around to face the direction of the noise. Screech, there it was again, louder this time. It sent a chill running down the length of her spine. A bird, it was the sound of a bird. The bird, the black bird that was at Mrs. Cartwright's. "It's a sign of death Martha, and I ignored it." Mrs. Cartwright's words rang rich in her ears. For a moment, Martha thought of running out of the house as fast as she could. Don't be silly, Martha, she said to herself. You are a grown woman, all these old wives' tales are getting to you. With all the bravery she could muster, she strolled out of the kitchen and turned to climb the stairs to Franky's room.

It had taken all day to get things rolling. First, the men had to decide what actions to take. Next, of course, came the shopping for those items they felt they would need to challenge the strong foe. Kip for instance had insisted on buying an axe. If worse came to worse, he would cut the bastard's head off. Philip had insisted on gas and book matches. It was Frank's belief that aerosol cans and lighters were the best weapon. By the time it was over, they had gone from store to store and bought all those items and much more. It had become apparent halfway through that Philip's MG would not be sufficient, so Kip rented a larger car that could carry the ever-increasing load. By the time they were finished, most of the day was gone. It was Philip who finally decided to get something to eat. "We have got to have some strength if we are going to do this," he said "We haven't had a bite all day."

They ended up stopping at a local diner. The service there was extraordinarily slow. The waitress, who forgot to put in their order, walked as leisurely as humanly possible. After an hour's wait, they started to get up and leave. Fortunately, out she came from the kitchen carrying their food. With no time to go anywhere else, they decided to stay and eat. They guzzled down their food, paid their bill, and even though the service was bad, Kip left two dollars on the table for a tip. He told himself not to, but it was not in his nature to stiff a waitress.

It was now nearing dark. The plan was set. Philip and Kip were taking his rental to St. Timothy's where they would meet with the priest that Kip had communicated with on the phone previously. He was away and would not return until that evening. If everything went well, Franky would soon be getting a phone call. Franky reached down and switched on the stereo of Philip's MG.

My Sweet Lord, My, My Sweet Lord / I really want to see you / I really want to see you Lord, but it takes so long my Lord.

Franky smirked. He should have known that Mr. Parker listened to that old stuff. He reached down to find a better station, but the words of George Harrison seemed comforting to him so he let it play on.

Franky pondered what kind of reception he would get at home. Looking back, he knew he should not have snuck out the way he did. He was sure his mother would be worried to death about him. That is the only reason he had asked to take the MG in the first place. First, however, he had made Philip promise that they would do nothing without him. He would simply make an excuse at home and sneak down to Philip's. Until that instant, one thought had yet to occur to Franky, and he began to grin. He was planning on driving up in Philip's car. How would he explain that? The answer was easy enough, park the thing at Philip's house and walk home, but with all that had happened, he knew if he had not taken the time to think, he would have merely parked it in his own drive. Franky got a chill. Don't let me slip up like this when we go after this thing, he thought. For the first time the realism of the whole situation was hitting home. This was not going to be a day in the park. He was risking his life here. Then the memory of Susan filled his mind. It was almost as if she had not died at all. He could see her smiling face the day they went looking for the apartment and the way she always took the time to talk before class. Yes, Franky knew what he was getting into alright, but he also knew why.

Martha Lake came to in a daze. Her eyes fluttered slowly open. She went to rub them but could not move her arms. She looked at her right arm and saw that it was wrapped up in an old rag. Giving another tug she noticed that it was in fact not wrapped, but tied, tied to an old bedpost. She looked around still in a haze and grasped she was no longer at home. This room was gloomy and peculiar to her. It had a thick, musty aroma to it. Martha laid her head back down and tried to think. The last thing she could recollect was walking up the stairs to Franky's room, how she had gotten here was a mystery. She turned to look at the other arm and it too was tied tightly to a bed post. What the hell is going on she thought? Had she fallen down the steps? Was she in the hospital? All sorts of thoughts came rushing through her mind. If she were laying on a bed, why was it so hard? She tried to turn her head to look around in the darkness but could see nothing but the bedpost.

The bird, she remembered hearing the sound of a bird in Franky's bedroom. She remembered going up the stairs, and then . . . nothing, she could remember nothing.

"Ssso, you are awake my dear," came a voice in the darkness.

Across the room, there was an oval porthole window which allowed just enough light for Martha to perceive the shape of a man moving toward her. It stopped just above her and bent over. She still could not make out the face or the voice.

Though disoriented, Martha at once realized that she was in abundant danger and began to scream at the top of her lungs.

"Ssscream all you want my dear, no one can hear you."

Martha heaved hard on the rags that bound her. She thought she felt one give slightly, she could have sworn she heard the faintest rip. She tried again, but nothing happened.

"Now, now my dear," came the voice from the darkness.

That voice, it was so pure, so kind and soft. Martha was sure if he kept talking she would be lost in his words.

"What the hell do you want from me.?" she yelled. Every nerve in her body was alive. She could feel every inch of her body fill with strength. She pulled once more on her straps. This time there was no doubt, she felt one giving way a little more.

"You are a fine looking wench."

Afraid that he could hear the old rags tearing, Martha, tried hard to control her new found strength and almost overwhelming fear. She eased up on the rags, slowly applying the pressure, so that the rag on the left that had started to tear, continued to do so, but at slower, quieter rate. Then, she felt him touch her. His hands were ice-cold as they ran up the length of her thigh.

"I will not kill you yet my dear. I need you to bring the othersss. However, in the meantime, maybe I can fill an urge as bad as my hunger.

Finally Martha felt the rag give way. Her left hand move slightly forward but she hurriedly pulled it back so that this asshole could not see that she had at least one hand free. This she would keep to herself until the time was right, until he was right where she wanted him. She could feel this body slowly sliding up hers, felt his huge icy erection as he rubbed it up against her inner calf.

Biting back fear, anger, hatred, and disbelief, she waited.

"You will enjoy thisss, I promissse you."

Slowly he lifted himself up to spread her legs. He went to remove her satin panties and that was when she made her move. She brought her knee up hard into his crotch. Though she could not see a thing, she had managed to find her mark, and Fritz went down hard on the floor. Quickly as she could, she reached over with her free hand an untied the other. With the speed of a cat she was on her feet running toward the only light she could find, the window. Maybe she could jump, or crawl out on the roof, something. But once she got there, she soon realized that she was far too high, there was no roof, and the fall would only kill her. She was not ready to die just yet. For the first time, she realized where she was, for the lake could be seen unmistakably. The old manor, she must be in the attic of the old manor.

"Not thisss time," she heard the voice behind her say. Fritz was getting to his feet.

Martha began to panic; the room was too dark to see any way out.

"You women in thisss world all fight alike, I may not bed you wench, but you will make me further whole," said Fritz. Slowly he came closer. "Do not struggle my precious, I will make you a deal."

Again, Martha became overwhelmed with his voice. She paused at its power. Then Fritz stepped into the last bit of evening light. There in the gloomy light, she saw him, half-man, half-beast. The entire left side of his body was ordinary, but the right looked like some creature out of a B horror movie. Skin so white, it seemed to shine in the light, it covered his torso like an old wrinkled blanket, not seeming to be attached to any muscle beneath. Where an arm and hand ought to be, there was long skin-covered bone with an enormous claw-like hand. His foot, or what appeared to be his foot, resembled a grotesque paw of some tortured animal. His manhood, long and what seemed to be painfully twisted now dangled half erect between his legs. Martha began to scream, but again he spoke.

"There, there my beauty, I mean you no harm."

Martha looked up into his face. Like his body, there was no symmetry, only confusing opposition, with half-human, even good looking, but the other was nothing more than a skull with a thin layer of pale skin. That's when it happened. Martha sealed her fate and looked directly into his eyes, those bright, beautiful, blue eyes.

After waiting what seemed to be an eternity, Kip and Philip were finally escorted down a long narrow corridor to the office of Father McMurry. There, he sat with his face to the wall, taking very little notice of them.

"Father, I don't know if you remember me or not, but I'm Kip, how are you doing?"

"Don't take this personally, but I was hoping you would not show up." Slowly, he turned his face to them. "Please have a seat, and your friend too."

"This is Professor Parker, from the college."

"Does he have a first name?"

"Philip," said Philip reaching out his hand. He was surprised by the firmness of the old man's grip.

"I am sorry for the wait, but as I told you on the phone I had some business to take care of this afternoon. I did not realize it would take so long."

"That's quite all right," said Kip as Philip nodded in response. Both at this instant were afraid to utter a word about what they wanted but neither had worried for the Priest started speaking at once.

"I take it the man they captured the other day was not the one they were really looking for."

"Well," said Kip ready to give an explanation.

"And you know when you find that man you are looking for, that he may not be a man at all and you are seeking my help to put an end to him."

"How do you know all this?" asked Philip no longer willing to remain silent.

"Because of this," came the answer, and the Priest held up an old stack of yellowed papers. "But before I tell all that I know, perhaps it would be best if you told me all that you know first. After all, I am about to give away information that has been guarded by this church for the past hundred and fifty-odd years."

Philip looked at Kip for approval and got it with a nod of his head. "Well, it all started with these dreams I was having . . ."

Franky returned home to an empty house. Jake's van was gone, and the only thing that Franky could think was that his mother and Jake were out there somewhere looking for him. As he walked around the silent house, he felt a weird sensation. The house felt changed somehow. It was if some element which had always been there, something that had made it seem so warm and comforting, was misplaced. He could not put his finger on it, but it was strange. A feeling of foreboding gloom fell upon him, and he sat there quietly in the dark at the kitchen table. Though the sun still cast a small glimmer from atop the trees, the house itself was filled with dark shadows and the little bit of light that did gleam through offered little for the eyes to see.

That is when he first heard the sound of wings close by. Franky sat there, listening without a sound. He wanted whatever it was to go away and leave him at peace. But leave him alone it did not. As he sat, a bird with plumage so dark it could scarcely be seen in the darkness, lit softly upon the table inches from his folded hands. Franky could do nothing but stare at it in wonder.

The bird began to squawk, and Franky noticed something strange in its voice. Words, hard to make out at first, then they came through loud and clear. It was the tender voice of a child, soothing, and innocent. "He has her, your mother, be aware that he has your mother, up there." Franky, shook his head in total disbelief. "Up there, where the sun never shines, he has her. Your mother."

This time Franky's eyes lit up with *your mother*. "You can help me and her."

Something deep inside of Franky snapped. With the strength and speed of some wild animal, he brought his fist down hard upon the feathered creature. The loud bang from the impact could be heard throughout the house.

The bird lay there twitching, then simply lay still.

At that exact moment, across town, Scotty Cooper opened his eyes. It was very bright, as the glow from the overhead light shined directly into his eyes. On his left, he could make out a man working at a desk. On his right stood a long cabinet filled with some sort of medical equipment. Where he was he was not sure, but one thing was for certain. He was back, back in the body from which he had come. He had faced the wrath of his master by warning the boy, in return, the boy had set him free. If only he had known all along that someone other could set him free, he would have never done the horrific things he had done. As he tried to rise, pain radiated from his chest through every inch of his body. My God, there was no coming back, it was all a lie, there was no returning, but he had promised if he did those unspeakable things, it was all a lie. Everything started turning gray. "Forgive me, my Lord," he said out load as everything went from gray to black.

Sam turned to the sound only to find Scotty collapsing back onto the table. He heard him, he heard him saying something, "Forgive me, my Lord," he heard it. And he had seen him move, he knew what he had seen, and he saw the boy move.

He flung himself up from this chair and ran to the boy. He grabbed his wrist, no pulse.

Sam stood there, his mouth opened wide, there was discoloration on the boy's skin, he rolled him over and he was like a bowl of jelly, "primary flaccidity" he said aloud, but within seconds he felt the muscles tighten, rigor mortis was setting in. It was impossible. This usually took hours. Sam was amazed and horrified all at the same time. All this time, the boy had defied the rules of nature by not dying and now within a minute, he was going through the stages of post-mortem. Sam knew this time, he was dead; Scotty Copper was truly dead. But he had seen him move, he had heard him speak, he was not hallucinating, it was real. Damn it, it was real.

Franky sat back in his chair and stared at the creature in the darkness, he shouldn't have. He was not at all surprised when the fowl once again stood, only this time its head lay limp to one side.

"Alone are we Franky, a little frightened maybe?" It spoke once more, only this time it was not the voice of a child, but that of Fritz, of that, Franky was sure.

"Where ever can those friends of yours be? Maybe they have forgotten about you. Maybe they are not even alive to help, have you thought about that? It doesn't really matter now, though, does it, for even they cannot help you, and God only knows who can help that sweet little mother of yours."

"If you have hurt her . . ."

"You will what?"

Franky now took another swing at the fowl creature but it quickly flew to the top of the refrigerator.

"You fool, you cannot harm what is already dead. You killed my pet already you little prick, now let's see if you can keep me from killing that bitch you call mother."

Quickly, the room was filled with light, shining through the kitchen window. Franky looked up in time to see the bird's twisted body tumble lifeless to the floor. The room then turned dark once again and Franky heard a car door slam. He ran to the window. It was Jake. He was making his way around to the house. By the time Jake reached the front door, Franky was on his way out. His face was as white as a sheet and the look on his face was one of distress and desperation.

"What the fu . . ." Jake began to say.

"I know who the killer is and he has mom," yelled Franky and then burst out into tears. "For God's sake, we have to help her."

"What, wait a minute, back up."

"Give me your keys, please, we have to get to her before . . ."

Jake reached out and grabbed the now hysterical Franky by the shoulders.

"We are not going anywhere until you calm down and tell me what the hell you are talking about."

Franky, who was now close to hyperventilating, tried hard to catch his breath. "Please, oh God, trust me on this one, if we do not leave right now, it may be too late."

Jake looked into Franky's terrified eyes. He had no idea what was going on, but one thing was absolutely clear, Franky was not making any of this up. "Okay, now slow down," said Jake in a calm, soothing voice. "Now, tell me who has Aunt Martha and where they are."

Franky let out a loud sigh at Jake's willingness to listen. "His name is Fritz, he is the one that has been doing all of the killing in Parksville." Franky now looked Jake square in the eyes so that he would know he was telling the truth. "I cannot tell you right now how I know this, but he has mom up at the old manor, I am sure of it."

Jake slowly released Franky's shoulders. "All right, we'll go up there, but I'm driving do you understand?"

"Yes, fine, whatever let's just go."

"First, I think we should call the police."

"No," shouted Franky, "they already know."

"You called them?"

"They know, you must believe me."

"All right, get in the van." No sooner did these words escape his lips. Then Franky flew to the van and shut the door. Jake, now feeling some urgency himself, followed suit.

Not a solitary word was spoken on the way. Jake did not know what to say or what to think. He was driving at a reckless pace when they came over the last hill overlooking the lake. The old manor could be seen looming in the distance. Then, without warning the lights caught the figure of a man standing right in the middle of the road. Jake could not stop or swerve. In fact, he had just enough time to reach for the brake before he heard a large thump against the front of the van. The man went soaring into the air and landed a distance twenty feet ahead. Franky's head went smashing into the windshield and Jake heard a loud crack. Jake finally managed to come to a skidding stop. He looked over at Franky. His head was bleeding and he sat back in the seat moaning.

"You all right, Franky, are you all right?"

Franky gave another moan.

"He came out of nowhere man, I swear, I never saw him."

Then Jake reached for the door handle, he had to see. For all he knew he had just killed some poor bastard. He had to see if he was alive. "I'll be right back man," he said, and left the van.

Franky lifted his head in time to see Jake walking over to the figure sprawled out on the dirt. Blood was running into his eyes and it stung. He watched as Jake leaned over the figure. That is when he came to his senses. He leaned out the open window and yelled, "No!" Then in an instant the figure rolled over and swung around a large claw that struck Jake in the throat. Blood gushed from Jake's jugular. Then before Jake even realized what had happen the claw vanished into his chest.

Franky watched as Fritz pulled hard then held his cousins heart over his head like a trophy. In the bright head lights he could see him grin as he pushed Jake's still twitching body to the ground. He rose and sauntered toward the van with the heart stretched out in front of him.

Franky screamed. He reached over and rolled up his window, then the driver's side. He had just pushed the lock when he saw Fritz through his window. Franky moved in time as Fritz's claw came smashing through the glass. Broken pieces flew everywhere. Fritz reached for him but Franky was too quick. The only thing that saved him was the fact that Fritz did not know how to unlock the door, he kept pulling on it, expecting it to open. This obviously had him quite distraught for he grabbed the van from the bottom and began to rock it. Franky mustered the last bit of courage he could and headed for the back doors. He swung one open and leaped out just in time as the van was flung over on its side. He could see Fritz standing there gaping at it as if in victory. Then he caught sight of Franky.

Franky got up and started to run up the road toward the lake. He could hear Fritz behind him. Flap, thud, Flap, thud as first his disfigured foot struck the road and then his good. The sound keep getting closer and closer, Franky was running as fast he could but the sound kept getting nearer and nearer. Franky knew that Fritz must be right on top of him, he could even sense his breath heaving on the back of his neck. He could smell its malicious odor. Franky's heart was pumping so fast that he thought that it was going to burst from his chest. Then Fritz would have two trophies. He would not give him that satisfaction. He turned to fight, but Fritz was not there. Nothing was there except empty road. He turned and looked at the lake, nothing there. Franky gave a sigh of relief, safe for the moment. He turned to walk back to the van, only he turned and walked directly into Fritz.

He felt something hit his head, then all was dark.

"Your story is quite remarkable, Mr. Parker," said Father McMurry.

Philip could not see any belief, or disbelief for that matter on the Priest's face. He had not interrupted once during his entire tale and was now simply staring at him with a blank face. No hint was there of his judgment. Slowly, he glanced down at the manuscript before him on his desk. "You say you have only seen this Fritz in your dreams, is that correct?"

"Yes," said Philip, all of this was now starting to get on his nerves and he could wait no longer. "Do you believe me or not?"

"Unfortunately, I believe every word. If you would have come to me and told me this tale a week ago, I would have called you insane. But I have proof to back up every word of this."

McMurry lifted the old manuscript. "This," he said pointing to the manuscript, "is the tale of one Father McDonald, the founder of St. Timothy's. If you allow me, I would like to give you a brief summary of what it says."

Both men nodded in agreement.

"The year was 1780. Father McDonald had just taken charge of a small parish outside of Dublin. According to the good Father he belonged to a secret order that, well, for lack of a better word, were witch hunters ordained by the Church. There had been rumors of strange activities in Dublin and it wasn't long until he heard gossip about a rich foreigner by the name of Banthom that lived in a large mansion overlooking the village. They say that he was a devil worshiper and that he was trying to recruit parishioners to his so called cult. Father McDonald was getting ready to confront the man, when he left the village, along with a number of local villagers for England. Parents and friends pleaded with the priest to help them get them back. McDonald agreed and set off for England. There, he would run into Banthom in London. McDonald traveled in secret, and since no one knew him by name or face, he joined Banthom's group in hopes of finding out what was going on. A Catholic Irish priest may be able to throw some weight around at home, but here he would need something solid to go on in order to get help.

For five months, he stayed with the band. Banthom was trying to build a cult, thirteen members, so that he could fill his dreams of becoming a true witch. McDonald learned that Banthom had in his possession, two ancient books that were said to be written by Satan himself. These books, identical in every way, contained the formula for gaining the powers of evil. First, they must follow a secret rite of passage. This involved a sacrifice of a virgin male and then the consumption of a virgin female's living flesh. In this way, the cult member was in fact selling his soul for eternal life, a life that can only be ended by flame."

"That's what I saw in my dream. That's why they were all burned alive." Philip interrupted.

"Please, let me finish," responded McMurry. "Once eternal life was bestowed, the final act was to have the high priest buried alive for three days, only then to be dug up, (or resurrected as it may be). Once arisen, they would need to repeat the ritual to become human in form. For, you see, they were only kept alive with the aid of evil and would start to resemble that evil. Only by stealing a piece of the human soul could the body heal itself. That can only be done through the consumption of living human flesh. Once whole, the high priest would have all the powers of evil at his command. Or so McDonald says."

"Man, that's sick stuff there, Father."

"Well, this is no game Mr. Gillmore. What we are dealing with is more than some slasher in a movie."

"How does Fritz fit in to all of this? Is he this Banthom guy, or what?"

"Well, the answer is here in his writings. Like I said, McDonald stayed with the group long enough to find out what was going on. When the cult was complete, the rituals actually started. He went at once to the authorities. They cornered the band in a pub. All fled except for one Lord Bacon. It seems that he was what they called the Judas, the thirteenth member. It was his job to take over for the high priest in case of his death to the flame. Only he could have possession of the second book, but when they found him it was not there. McDonald demanded that they burn him on the spot, and they did without question. It seems that one of the children used in their first ritual was no other than a niece of a local official."

"Anyway, it took McDonald and his new band of soldiers a year to find them once again. In an open field, just across the border in Scotland, they hunted them down, just as they were anointing a new Judas."

"Fritz, I saw the whole thing," stated Philip.

"I believe you did," answered Father McMurry.

"Most of them were burned alive, two members got away. Banthom and Fritz. McDonald at once was on their heels. He tracked Banthom back to his home in Ireland, but when he got there, Banthom was not to be found. McDonald was certain that the villagers, hearing of the death of loved ones in England, dealt with Banthom in their own way. McDonald tried to find out what they did with the body, but fearing repercussions, they would not admit to the crime or give him any information. He could only hope that they had burned him, for if he was killed in any other way, he would have faked his death and would still be alive, waiting to be resurrected. If this happened, he would be more powerful than anyone could imagine."

"McDonald then had a decision to make. Either stay there and look for Banthom and his books, or track down Fritz. With all of his followers gone, and with the villagers' complete silence, hopefully Banthom would never be found. He at once contacted the head of his secret order and told them of his actions and what to do if they saw signs of Banthom's return; he would keep them informed of his progress when he could, and then he took off in search of Fritz. He would never find out what really happened to Banthom or what the villagers did with the body."

"McDonald tracked Fritz to America. It took nearly a life-time to locate him, but in the year 1840, at the age of 81, Father McDonald followed the trail to what is now the town of Parksville. There he ran into a man who had worked as Fritz's male servant. The man described a man by the name of Smith who had pure white hair, even though he did not look a day of twenty. He claimed that he lived in the large manor by the lake and that he was always chatting about starting a new race, one in which he would have supreme power. The man stated that he had even tried to recruit him to become a cult member. When word got out what he was up to, the towns people, like the villagers in Ireland, dealt with the matter. Two prominent members of the community, a Joshua Parker and an Adam Wells, gathered a lynch mob and went after him. They hung him from a large oak tree, then buried him just outside of the old cemetery."

"Joshua Parker was my ancestor, he was the one that founded Parksville." said Philip.

"McDonald speaks very kindly of him and this Mr. Wells. Maybe that is why you were chosen," answered McMurry.

"If that's the case, then why Franky? His last name is Lake."

"I don't know," answered McMurry.

"I do," said Kip. "I was stupid for not making the connection earlier. It's so damn obvious."

Both men stared at Kip in wonderment.

"Franky Lake, Frank Lake, it was right there in front of me. I knew a Frank Lake years ago. He was from Ohio and moved here to find work. Good looking guy. He and his brother in-law, Jake I think his name was, anyway they were both killed in a plane crash a long time ago. All of us bowled on the same league for years. He married a girl from Springport, oh what was her name?"

"Martha," said Philip.

"Yeah, that's it, Martha, Martha Wells. She and her husband moved to Parksville around the time you left for college as I remember. Nice people."

"Well that solves that mystery," said McMurry obviously trying to finish his tale. "Getting back to the story. McDonald went to the cemetery and found the unmarked grave. All those years he had tracked this man down only to find him here. At his age, he knew that he could not dig up Fritz. If the stories were all true, then Fritz did not truly die at the end of a rope. He would still be living under the earth. The priest knew he was too old and that Fritz would be too powerful to deal with.

"In the old manor, McDonald found this book. There was no question that this was in fact Fritz. So with nothing else to do, Father McDonald moved here to Jackson, founded St. Timothy's, waited and watched. That's when he started working on this manuscript. There are parts obviously omitted, I presume they were meant for his order back home. He also started studying this," the Priest pointed to the old black book. "He says in his writings that it was so evilly conceived that it almost drove him insane and he had to stop in fear of his losing his soul.

"Just before he died, he had two stone lions added to the gates of the old cemetery. Feeling guilt for his own weakness, he states that he prayed that if anyone was to release the malicious spirit, that the lions would see and beckon him from beyond the grave to help combat this monster."

Father McMurry looked at the two men sitting there. "Of course, most of us who have read this manuscript thought that the man was insane when he wrote it. I was one of them. This book however, you can almost feel its evilness. I looked at it once. It is written in Latin. Only this book is written from end to beginning. I got such a bad feeling from it, I put it down and never looked at it again."

"Look, we have got to kill this thing," said Philip, "In my dreams the priest prayed while the bodies were burning. We need you to do the same. Can you help us?"

"I will help you, but first I need to know, do you believe in God?"

Philip looked thoughtfully at the priest, this was no time for a lie. "I don't know," he said, "I don't think I do, no."

"You will," answered the priest "and you must."

"Well what are we waiting for?" exclaimed Kip. He had been silent long enough. "If we are going to do this, then let's get it done."

"First I must pray in the chapel if that is alright. I am not a young man, and I need God to give me strength."

With that, the three men got up. Following the priest down a long hallway, they walked into the chapel of St. Timothy's. It was beautiful, with large stained glass windows and statues of saints standing tall above them. At the altar, the Priest knelt and started whispering a prayer while Kip and Philip stood close by and watched.

Philip looked around. They were the only ones there.

"Do not worry," said McMurry, "it cannot enter here."

Suddenly the large mahogany door burst open with a loud boom. The windows in the church all at once exploded inward and a squall blew through the church with a gale type force. McMurry lost his balance and fell hard to the floor.

"Be gone! Be gone!" screeched McMurry, holding his bible high. "You have no power here. Now in the name of God, be gone."

The wind did not subside and they could hear the church creak and crack as if the entire building would collapse around them at any moment.

"In the name of the Father, the Son, and the Holy Ghost I command you to leave." The priest rose to his knees.

Trash from the street started rushing through the open door.

"This is the house of our Lord, be gone."

"The door began to slam shut, then open, then shut, over and over again. The noise it made was deafening.

"In the name of the creator, I command you, be gone!" the priest yelled at the top of his lungs, still barely audible over the all-encompassing banging.

As fast as it had all started the wind stopped, and there was sudden calm.

Kip and Philip stood looking at each other. McMurry, still on his knees, had no look of fear, but of defiant determination.

"He is here," said Kip. "He must have followed us."

"No," said the Priest, "he is not here, he could be anywhere, but he would not dare fight us on sacred ground. His powers are strong, maybe too strong. He could be anywhere. He could be doing this from the manor for all we know. I must finish getting my things. This has got to be done tonight."

"I think we have everything we need," said Kip.

"I rely on the weapons of our Lord," said the priest. He got up, filled a small bottle of holy water then walked over and retrieved his bible. "Now I am ready," he stated.

"Wait, first I have to make a phone call," said Philip.

Franky had no idea how long he had been out. When he first started to come to, the only thing he knew for sure was that his head hurt. He did not really understand that he now had two gashes, one on each side of his head, for the pain seemed to mingle and meet at the top of his skull. His first thought was that of a football game he had watched once when the Bears had played the Lions in a close game. Two Bears had run through the line like they were not even there and sandwiched the quarterback, one hitting him high and one hitting him low. It was Eric Hipple if memory served him right. Anyway, it had amazed him when Hipple had hopped back up and finished the game. Now he knew how that must have felt.

Franky got up and looked around. It took a minute for his eyes to focus in the darkness of the room. The moon was shining full through the window and he knew at once where he was. Once, when he was a child his father had brought him here. He was in the attic of the old manor. That was when his father had dreams of buying this land, knocking down this house, and building his dream house. That now seemed a life-time ago.

He observed that he had been leaning against the door, and at once went for the knob wanting to get out of there as soon as he possibly could. The knob, however would not turn, it had been locked from the outside. A horrible thought came rushing through Franky's aching head. He quickly looked around to see if the creature was in the room with him. In a panic, his eyes surveyed the entire room. He saw nothing lurking in the dark shadows, nothing but a set of old bed posts with rags tied around them and an old trunk sitting in the corner. Franky gave a sigh and then remembered what happened last time he thought it was safe. That damn creature must have carried him up here, but why. Why was he still alive?

A shiver ran down his spine as the recollection of Jake's heart in that outstretched hand came rushing back. He sat back down, his head was screaming with pain and he felt for sure that he would again pass out. He sat there thinking. He knew that Fritz was not around. He knew it. He could feel it. Still, the question of why he was still alive preoccupied him. Maybe it could not kill him; maybe the priest was able to protect him; maybe someone else had shown up at the very last minute; maybe something came up that it needed to deal with first. But still the creature had managed to bring him up here. Why? He remembered the dream where he first saw Fritz. Was he saving him because he was a virgin, was he wanting to do the same ritual as before? Was he to be his final sacrifice? Why else did he simply kill Jake without even taking the time for a meal? Is that why he had locked him here in this room, until the time was right and the moon was full? Then it hit him, bait. He was bait, just as his mother had been bait. Mom, thought Franky.

He could not take it any longer. He started pounding his shoulder against the door, but it did not budge. It was an old solid oak door and someone had taken pains to see that when this door was locked, it was locked good and tight. Franky reached into his pockets looking for something to pick the lock, but his pockets were empty. Maybe if he had something to pry it open with. He looked around. The bedpost. He stumbled over to the east wall and went to grab one of the heavy wooden post but they would not budge. Franky quickly realized that they were nailed to the wall. Why anyone would nail bedpost to the wall was beyond him but then again, this was not your average house to begin with.

He grabbed ahold of one and began to pull with all his might. His head was pleading with him to stop but all of the sudden he felt the old rotten boards give and he went down hard on his butt. He sat there for a while holding on to the bedpost that was now in his hand, and waited for his mind to clear. Pain seemed to be everywhere. When finally he felt he could walk again, he got up and half dragged the bedpost to the door. He gave it all he could and sent the bed post smashing into the door. Nothing, nothing but pain, instant and almost overwhelming. He knew he could not muster another swing, he must find another way. Then he thought of the trunk in the corner. Maybe something to pick the lock, an old hat pin or hair clip, something.

He staggered slowly over to the chest. He reached for the lid but it would not move. At first he thought it too was locked, but he gave it another try to make sure. He heard the old metal hinges give a little, so he lifted as hard as he could. Wham, the lid went flying and hit the wall with a bang. It took a moment for Franky to realize what he was looking at in the moonlight. Then the room was filled with his screams. There looking up at him was Martha. Her eyes wide open, gazing out of a sunken blue tinted face. Her body was stained red with blood. She had been gnawed in half and placed in the trunk in two sections. The upper torso lay neatly on top of her legs and hips. Franky reached over and slammed the lid down hard. His eyes started to swell and tear, his vision blurred. It wasn't real. Fritz was having some fun with him, that's all. He began walking backwards away from the trunk. "God knows who can help that sweet little mother of yours." The bird's words came back to him and hit him like a boulder. He could not get her face out of his mind, the way her eyes seemed to stare at him.

His foot caught the side of the bedpost he had used on the door as he was walking blindly backwards. He lost his footing and came dropping backward on the floor, his head gave a loud thud as it hit and then once again, all was dark.

Halfway to Parksville, Philip was giving a mental check in his head. There were two five-gallon cans of gas now riding safely in the trunk of the rental along with Franky's aerosol cans and Kip's axe. "That should be enough to get the bastard burning" Kip said to Philip when he paid the pimple faced cashier, who in turn gave him a peculiar look. Somehow, Philip still was not sure. He looked into the back seat and gave the Priest a look. He was reading from the Bible and gave him no notice. Philip checked his pockets. There were two Bic lighters, in his pants and two packs of matches. Then he reached down on the floor and the six empty beer bottles were still there for they gave a small click. In between were the rags.

"Would you just relax?" said Kip. "Everything is ready." He was driving as fast as he could for the night had started to get foggy and the road had just enough mist to make his lights shine on the wet pavement then vanish a few yards ahead of him.

"I wish I could be sure," said Philip. "I have a bad feeling about all of this." If only Franky would have been there when he called. Where could he be? Philip knew Franky would not just sneak off and leave them to fight this monster on their own. And why didn't Martha or Jake pick up. "The first thing we need to do is find Franky," said Philip, "I don't know why, but I don't think we can do this without him."

Kip turned to flash him a look, that's when it happened. Out of nowhere a guy was standing right in the middle of the road. Before Kip could react, the man disappeared under the car and he could hear a thump, thump as the tires rolled over him.

Kip slammed his foot on the brakes and started to pull over to the side of the road. "Shit!" was the only word he could find to use.

"No," cried Father McMurry, "do not stop. It is him I know it. Take off, we cannot face him here you fool, we are not ready, take off."

Slowly Kip released the brake and the car continued to roll. Kip looked out his back window at the shape lying there. Sure enough, the figure stood up when he saw that the car would not stop. It started running for them. Kip slammed the gas pedal to the floor. The tires began to spin on the wet pavement and then grabbed ahold and sent them lunging forward.

It was McMurry that gave the warning, "look out!" as Fritz gave one final bound for the car and landed on the trunk lid. He grabbed the window trim with his good hand and sent his claw smashing into the back window. The glass fractured but did not give. Kip began to swerve, trying desperately to shake him off, but Fritz held tight. He gave another blow and this time the claw went straight through, the entire back window gave way and glass came hurtling inward. Before he could react, McMurry felt Fritz's grip upon his throat. Philip could see what was happening but did not know what to do. Fortunately McMurry did. As fast as lightning McMurry reached into his pocket and grabbed a bottle he had there. He reached out and handed it to Philip. Philip grabbed the vile and pulled off the lid with his teeth. Then he realized he did not know for sure what to do with it, he did the only thing he could think of, he threw it at Fritz's claw. The liquid inside, landed on its mark and the skin covering the claw began to fizzle. Philip heard a loud shout and then saw the claw give way. Philip watched as Fritz went rolling off the back of the car and down the road. For a second, he thought he saw him stand up again as if to give another chase, but then simply vanished into the darkness. Philip looked at McMurry. He was praying. Philip noticed that he had not escaped totally unharmed for there was a nasty scratch on his neck that was bleeding. McMurry stopped praying and looked at Philip. "Holy water," he said, pointing to the empty bottle Philip was still holding.

"How did you know?"

"You are one that studied the past without believing in all of its mysteries. I am one that studies those mysteries and knows them to be true," answered McMurry. Then he pulled a hanky from his pocket and wiped the blood from his neck. "It's not all that bad," he mumbled and put the hanky back in his pocket and returned to his bible. Philip got the hint, he checked once more to make sure that Fritz was not there and then turned around. He sat there without speaking for a long time.

Franky opened his eyes. He lay quietly. Murkiness seemed to clear from his mind and the pain, though still strong, was buried deep within him. Looking around the room, he somehow found it more immense, more eerie than before, as if the devil himself had given it his personal touch, placing unseen demons behind every rafter and in every darkened corner. The moon seemed to have all but gone out, for the ray did not shine as brightly through the small round window. It was vague.

Creak, came the sound from the far corner where the trunk rested. Creak. Once more.

Franky turned his head half-expecting to see Fritz's evil grin looking back at him, but there was no one there, not even a small mischievous goblin. There was only the trunk and its lid slowly coming open. Franky felt the urge to scream, but fear would not allow him the luxury. Though the night had begun to chill with the fog, Franky broke out in a sweat, as inch by squeaking inch the lid continued to rise.

Gradually, a bluish hand appeared from inside the trunk and grabbed the lid. It threw it up hard, causing it to crash against the wall behind it. Franky could not only hear the impact, but he felt it, down to his bones. Paralyzed with his own fear, he could not move. Slowly a second hand clawed its way to the top edge of the trunk. It, however, was not blue, but covered in bright red blood that dripped with a magnified splat on the old wooden floor.

Franky tried to move. He tried to scream, but all he could do was lay there in shock and watch.

Watch as slowly but surely his dead mother pulled herself upright and glared straight into his eyes.

"Why didn't you help me Franky, why?" pleaded Martha. Her hair was matted and tainted with blood and her face appeared thinner, as if the very life had been sucked out of it. "Why did you let that foul creature touch me?"

Franky began to cry, it was the only thing his mind would permit him to do. Loud sobs of agony filled the room. He tried to close his eyes, to look away, but he could not. They were fixed on hers and they were full of confusion and horror. "Why?"

"My God, what did he do to you?" Franky babbled in reply. "You're dead. Leave me alone. I tried to help, I tried. So please, for God sakes, leave me alone."

Martha grabbed the side of the chest and lifted herself up, then bent over the top. With a loud thud, the top half of her mutilated body came crashing onto the floor. She landed on her face and chest. Within an instant, she had put her hands flat on the floor, and lifted herself up so that she was once again, eye-to-eye with Franky.

Franky, gaining some control, sat up and started to scoot backward, away from her. He unknowingly had released body fluids down his pants and onto the floor.

Martha began using her arms to drag herself along, leaving behind a dark trail of blood. She started heading straight for Franky.

"It is all right now baby," she muttered. "Come, let Momma make everything alright." She stopped, propped herself up with one arm and held out her other hand for him to take.

"No, you are not my mother," screamed Franky at last. "Get away from me"

"Why are you afraid of me, I am your mother, the one who has always loved you." Just then a huge brown spider fell from somewhere in the rafters. It landed squarely on Martha's face. She took no notice. "Please, Franky, I need your help." The spider crawled across her eye, over her ear, and into her hair.

"I love you, Franky." Once again, she started to crawl toward him, her eyes begging for him to come close.

"You are not my mother," yelled Franky. "You are a demon from hell, now leave me the fuck alone!"

Martha stopped dead in her tracks. For an instant it looked as if she would start to cry, then it came, laughter, loud hideous and deep laughter. "You fucking little nerd," she screamed at him in a bottomless male voice.

Franky jumped at the sudden change.

Martha's face started changing into that of half snake, half human. An evil creature from the very bowels of hell could not have been so vile. She gave him a loud hiss and then, without warning, an enormous red forked tongue shot from her mouth. He moved just in time as it whipped into the wall next to him. As quickly as she lashed it, the creature retrieved it and then struck again, and again a near miss. She smiled an ominous grin. "You will rot in hell just like that whore mother of yours," it hissed. With that, the creature made a mad rush straight toward him. Franky had just enough time to close his eyes and put up his hands, preparing himself for the inevitable blow.

It never came. After a few minutes, Franky opened his eyes, the creature was gone. The trunk was right where it had been, the lid was still closed, there were no blood tracks on the floor. The room looked just like it had before.

Thud, Thud, Thud, came the noise beyond the locked door. Someone was coming up the steps.

Thud, Thud, Clump, it had reached the top.

Fun and games are over, thought Franky. He has finally come for me. With that, he heard a click as someone outside turned the lock.

THURSDAY

Mrs. Cartwright jumped at the sound of the clock in the hallway striking the midnight hour. She had fallen asleep even though she was trying so hard to stay awake. Every light in the house was shining bright. In her lap sat a loaded twenty two, around her neck was a cross, and in her right arm was the Bible. She didn't care what the news said, the weirdo they arrested was not the one. She didn't know why she felt this way, but she knew it. Maybe it was the fact that she knew Jimmy and his mother. They were both strange enough, that was sure, but somehow it didn't feel right. It was as if something bigger was going to happen.

Slowly, she got up from her chair and walked into the kitchen. Looking from her window, she saw the Lakes' House with all the lights on. See, she was not the only one afraid. She never remembered seeing their lights on this late. Crossing the kitchen, she walked into the dining room where she had left her glasses. No sense having a bible if you weren't going to read it, and to tell the truth, it had been a long time since she had read from the Bible. But times were now dire.

There was a war coming, but without tanks or planes. A war between good and evil fought on some plane of existence, some unknown dimension and spilling over into this world. Living in New Orleans, she had seen a lot of things. Ethel Johnson, one of her dearest friends knew about these things. She knew about voodoo, black magic, spells, and potions. How she wished she was here right now, she would know how to ward off this malevolent spirit.

Brandy wasn't sure what was coming, but something was, and whatever it was, she sought to be ready.

"Franky, Franky are you in there?" came the call from outside the door.

Franky clinched his fist tight. The voice was familiar, but Franky no longer trusted any of his senses. From under the door, a gleam of light forced itself in to the darkened attic.

The door slowly began to open. The room began to fill with brightness that stung his eyes. Then he saw him, Philip, standing in the door way holding a flashlight.

Franky stood and threw himself into Philip's arms. Holding on for dear life, a loud excruciating sob burst forth.

Philip didn't know what to do. After leaving the Lakes' empty house and not finding him there, after searching his own house and not finding him there, his only hope, was that he would be here and alive. That hope drained when they saw the van and Jake's lifeless body. He wanted so desperately to ask about Martha, to find out where she was, if she knew, but he knew he would get no answer. Finally, he half dragged, half carried, the boy down three sets of stairs, to the enormous room where the others were waiting.

Franky never uttered a word and seemed to take no notice of Kip or McMurry. Philip laid the boy down on the floor where he sat motionless. Kip walked over and at once took off his jacket and put it around the boy. "He's in shock," he said. "Poor bastard, God only knows what he's gone through."

McMurry then walked over and, putting his hand on Franky's shoulder, looked him straight in the eye. "My boy, you have faced pure evil and lived to talk about it, now tell us what happened, all of it."

"For God's sake, leave the boy alone. He can't help us," said Philip.

"He's already been through hell."

"Yes, yes he has, but we have to know how strong the creature is, what he can do with his powers, how human he is."

"That's a bunch of shit," said Kip, "We know how strong he is, look at what he did back on the road."

"I do not think you do," came a weak voice. It was Franky. He swung around and knocked McMurry's hand off his shoulder. Suddenly his entire body started to shake. He was throwing his head back and forth violently, going beyond points that were humanly possible. Then he came to a dead stop. Still in a sitting position, he began to rise off the floor. The rest could do nothing but watch in disbelief. Hovering over their heads his eyes rolled back so far that they seemed to disappear, leaving only whiteness. He turned his head downward toward them. From nowhere a gust of stench fill wind came rushing through, sending long settled dirt and dust hurling through the air and into their burning eyes. "You have no idea of my power yet," came Fritz's voice from the mouth of Franky, "but you will. I have you where I want you. And you, priest," he laughed, "you were the best they could find?" The fowl creature laughed again in a voice so brash it echoed off the walls and a pain of glass in the old French doors shattered. Once again, Franky's infiltrated body began to shake and blood suddenly gushed from Franky's mouth and landed squarely on top of McMurry's head. "There, I baptized you in the name of the unholy spirit you pathetic fool," he spouted, wiping the blood from his chin. "You can't stop me. You never could."

McMurry wiped off his forehead. He looked up at Franky. "Your powers are no match for our Lord's. If you don't believe me, come and face me yourself you cowardly bastard."

With that the flashlights flickered off then on, the wind stopped blowing, and Franky came crashing to the floor. Philip ran over to him, he was out cold. Gently he laid his head in his lap and started stroking his forehead. Tears were coming to his eyes. After all he must have been through and now this. Philip felt something stir inside him. This fight was no longer something he dreaded. He wanted it. He had never felt such loathing, such a willingness to kill. The sooner the better he thought. Unfortunately, he would have to wait.

While Philip comforted Franky, the other two men at once started unloading the car. They had pulled right up the hill, as far as they could. Each one keeping a watchful eye, but there were no signs of Fritz. McMurry figured that even he could not have traveled as fast as they had in the car. Even with the stops they made, it would still take some time. Unless he had the power of flight or the ability to alter time, which he highly doubted.

Once the car was unloaded, they placed the still unconscious Franky in the middle of the room. They had spent some time debating if Franky needed to be removed from the house and taken some place safe, or even a hospital. They had agreed that separating the group at this point in the game was too hazardous; it may have been what Fritz was waiting for. Finally, they decided that Franky would stay, but they agreed to put him where they could all keep a better watch over him and laid him on the floor in the middle of the room.

The plan was simple. They would lure Fritz into the big room. They had carefully poured gas at its four entrances. The French doors, the stairway, the hall leading to the rest of the house, and the large opening where Kip had made his great escape. Once Fritz was in the room they would ignite all of the exits but one with the beer bottles that were now filled with gas and a small gas soaked rag, a Molotov cocktail. They would flee, lighting the remaining one on their way out. The aerosol cans they would use for fighting up close. Kip, of course still had his gun. It may not kill him, but it may slow him down. He also kept with him his axe. He figured if push came to shove, he would make the bastard fight without a limb, or maybe without a head if he got a good swing at it. Finally, they put what was left of the gas in a small bucket in case of an emergency. Once Fritz was trapped in the flames, McMurry would start to pray, and hopefully this thing would come to an end.

All was in place, the only thing to do now was wait. And wait they did. Minutes soon turned into hours, and still there was no sign. With every little noise, their hearts jumped only to find out it was a rat scurrying along, or the wind causing the old house to creak.

As they waited in the darkness, they silently disputed the cause for the wait. McMurry held to the belief that Fritz was still walking to get there, Kip argued that he would not show, he was afraid to face them all at once. Philip, however, had the opinion that he was already there, watching, studying, waiting for them to squirm until they were mentally and physically exhausted. Sooner or later they would make a mistake. Then and only then would he attack.

As time dragged on and daybreak drew near, it seemed to the group as if Kip had been right all along. Finally, McMurry got up and walked toward the opening in the wall.

"What are you doing?" questioned Philip.

"I need to relieve myself," answered McMurry.

"Okay, but stay where we can see you," added Kip

None of the group looked up to see the hidden shadow clinging silently to the ceiling. Up there, beyond the glow of the flashlights Fritz had been waiting, waiting for his chance. He now saw it. With the speed of an over grown cockroach, he slithered across the ceiling and down the wall. Kip spied him at last, but it was too late.

McMurry was undoing his fly when he heard Kip scream. He turned to see Kip pointing looking straight above his head. He looked up and stared into the eyes of Fritz. It was too late to react. Fritz's claw came crashing down on the side of his head. The force was so great, that it snapped McMurry's neck like a twig. He stood there for a moment, his head laying on his shoulder, then simply slumped to the floor. Kip, acting on instinct, grabbed his axe and sent it flying through the air at Fritz's head. Fritz, scampered out of the way, but not soon enough, for the axe missed his head but hit his wrist, just above the claw. The axe stuck in the wall but Fritz dropped to the floor, his body one way and his now severed claw the other. In a split second, Fritz, hopped to his feet and sprinted over to retrieve his appendage. He turned as he ran and glared at Kip. As quick as lightning he collected his claw and flung it directly at Kip. It soared through the air, fingers out stretched, and landed on Kip's throat where it grabbed hold and started choking him. Philip ran over and tried desperately to pull it off, but it was too strong. It clung to Kip like a vise, nails digging deeper and deeper into his skin. Kip struggled for air, staggered back and forth, while Philip, unwilling to give up, yanked with all his might. It seemed like an eternity, Kip continued to struggle, fight for his life, not willing to give in. As hard as he fought, Phillip fought harder, but it was for naught. Finally the battle was over, Kip gazed at Philip with terror in his eyes, then simply went limp, the life choked out of him.

With its mission complete. The claw eventually let loose and fell to the floor. Like some kind of deformed arachnid, it lifted itself on its fingertips and scurried across the floor toward the waiting Fritz. Just before it reached its destination, it flung itself into Fritz's waiting arms. Fritz took it and placed it back on his arm where it belonged. It seemed to smoke for a moment as it reattached itself, and soon it appeared as if nothing had happened. Fritz looked at Philip and grinned.

Philip gave a defiant growl, then made a mad dash for the French doors, he did not even attempt to open them, but went crashing through them like some stunt man in an action movie. He landed sprawled out on the patio outside. Philip looked up and sure enough, Fritz was right behind him, making his way through the now wide opening. Just as Fritz put his second foot on the old stones, Philip saw Franky out of the corner of his eye. He was holding a bucket, and before Philip could sort things out in his mind, Franky had drenched Fritz with the emergency gasoline.

Fritz's attention now turned to Franky, with one quick motion he picked him up with his claw and launched him across the night sky. Franky flew a good forty yards before he hit a pine tree down by the lake. Philip could hear the thud, as Franky first hit, then slid down the tree. There he lay motionless.

Philip wasted no time, from his pocket he grabbed a book of matches. As quickly as he could, which seemed an entirety with his shaking hands, he opened it, pulled off a match, turned the cover

over and struck it on the back. Fritz had already made his leap for Philip and hit him with the force of a truck. Unfortunately, for Fritz, he also hit the now burning match. Philip went flying backwards through the air with the impact of the blow; he landed hard on the ground. Looking up he saw that Fritz was engulfed in flames.

Philip shrieked, for the burning Fritz was walking toward him, laughing.

The prayer, with McMurry dead, there was no one to say the prayer. If only Philip had some faith, some belief in God. Then a feeling of calm came over him. Though he denied it all these years, it was there. With all that had happened he knew it to be true. With Fritz only a few feet away, Philip got to his knees and started saying the only prayer he knew.

"Our Father who art in Heaven,"

"No!" screamed Fritz.

"Hallowed be thy name."

All at once Fritz's body seemed to burn twice as brightly.

"Thy kingdom come, thy will be done"

Fritz started to yell and run around the patio in a panic, his foot caught on a loose stone and he went crashing into the wall of the house. The gas they had poured earlier by the French doors now exploded into flames and in an instant the manor was engulfed.

"On Earth as it is in Heaven"

Philip looked up again, and Fritz walked out into the grass, his skin peeling off in black embers that floated into the night sky.

"And give us this day"

With that, there was a large explosion and Fritz's body flew apart leaving only a glowing sphere of light that hovered just above the ground. From its interior tiny orbs of light emerged. They hovered over the sphere until, from the distant trees there came an apparition, it was Martha and she was smiling. One of the small orbs flew to her and as it touched her out stretched hand, she merely disappeared. Then came Big Bill, the Gibsons, and all those who had a part of their soul ripped from their bodies by Fritz. As soon as they recaptured the missing part of their soul, they were gone. Gone to a better place, thought Philip. When all had come and gone, Philip looked back at the sphere of light. Now it was the apparition of a young handsome man with long blonde hair and bright blue eyes.

It looked around, frightened. It attempted to soar across the field but was immobilized in midair. Philip watched it struggle to move, but it could not. The ground suddenly began to quiver. Philip went running to the safety of the trees, but before he could make it halfway, there appeared before him, directly under Fritz, a dark cloud of swirling smoke. In the middle, flames danced and twisted in long tall columns. It grew larger and larger, until it was the size of a baseball field.

Then, slowly from its center, a gigantic red claw, with long fingers, and coal black nails, came up from under the earth itself. Up, up it went until it reached Fritz's floating soul. Then, with a quick gesture, it snatched it out of the sky. A scream, so loud that Philip was forced to his knees. He covered his ears, as it bolted through the night sky.

Then, in an instant, the hand, the cloud, and the flames, vanished back into the ground. Philip, still on his knees, started crying. All the emotions one could feel in a lifetime came surging through his body. Unexpectedly, a hand landed with a loud slap on his shoulder. He turned to see Franky's blood-covered face. Still standing inches from the humongous burn hole in the earth, the two embraced. They held each other tight as over their shoulders the sun was casting its first rays over the treetops. It was the beginning of a brand new day.

Parksville 1998

Time passes, years seem only moments ago. At least that is what Philip thought as he downed his cup of coffee. Franky entered through the front door, it was a new Franky, a more mature Franky, but deep down he was the same individual he had always been.

"I loaded the car, I think I got everything."

"Okay. Thanks."

"I also called the hotel and they said that our reservations were confirmed, so at least we have a place to stay tonight."

"Great, then I think we are ready."

"Well I've got to drain the main vain, it's a long way to Metro."

"Alright, you do that." Phillip smirked.

Franky had moved in a few months after the gruesome tale was over. The only time he returned to the Lakes' house after that was to place the rest of his things into storage. Too many memories were in that house for him and Philip was glad to have him.

Before the fire department and cops arrived that early morning, the two men, leaving behind the rental car, returned home. They knew they could never say a word about what really took place, if they did, they would be implicating themselves in a mass murder, and there was little doubt that they would occupy the rest of their lives in prison.

The town had become a media circus with most of the attention on Sue Barkley, it was only then that the duo realized how influential her family truly was, and how well off she herself had been. TV crews were everywhere, on the streets they would detain anyone they saw to question them about the Parksville Massacre. Were they afraid to leave their house? Did they know the victims? How could such a diabolical event happen in their all-American hometown? Unfortunately, their principle target was Mrs. Cartwright, who could not even venture to escape her home for fear of being hounded by the press.

The FBI had interviewed Franky unremittingly over the next few days. How did Franky get the gashes on his head and bruises all over his body, (fell off my bike); what was his relationship to Kip Gilmore? (don't know who that is); did he know Father McMurry? (not at all) did his cousin say anything about why he was going to the lake? (didn't see him that night, never mentioned the lake or the manor); did he know why his mother had gone up to the mansion? (no idea). Phillip too, got his share of interrogation: why did you visit the captain in the hospital? (to see an old friend); what did you know about Sue Barkley's fortune? (she never mentioned it); were the two of you having an affair? (absolutely not). On and on came the boundless number of questions.

The story was simple, Professor Parker had spent the night tutoring young Mr. Lake for an upcoming examination and neither had any idea of what was going on in the world around them. Simple as that. And while both were sure there were many doubts as to the validity to their story, without a shred of evidence they knew the police could do nothing.

As for the manor itself, it was completely gone. The county finally purchased the land from the Gibson estate and decided to put in a park along the lake. Where the manor once stood there now were swings and a teeter-totter. All the brush has been cleared away down to the lake where there is now a nice, sandy beach. The spot of grass that was burned by the giant claw never grew back. It is nowadays used for little league baseball. It seemed so ironic to Philip that a place that once conveyed such agony could now convey such cheerfulness.

As the years passed, Franky graduated from P.U. and became a professor himself, teaching English Literature. He had dated numerous girls, some that Philip really did not approve of, but never seemed to get close to any of them. As for Philip, his dating days were over. Research had become his bride.

It took some time, but Philip had finally gotten his hands on the manuscript and black book from St. Timothy's. He befriended a young priest by volunteering as an assistant football coach. Finally, he got his chance and stole both works from the parish archives. The priest always supposed that he did it, but could not prove it. McMurry was right about one thing: he could only read so much of the black book at a time. It ate at your mind. He stopped after a short time. Besides, trying to translate with a guidebook was proving too difficult.

As for Mrs. Cartwright, she finally gave in and sold her house. Even after the media had faded away, gawkers were forever stopping in front of her house, it had become the legendary haunted house of Parksville. Tales of Sue Barkly walking the grounds at night in a white dress, and so on and so on. She still writes them both every now and then from Florida, where she still lives alone. Phillip is not sure, but he thinks Franky has confided their gruesome ordeal to her, breaking their code of silence, and he was okay with that. She had helped them both so much after it was all over. She helped Franky sell the house, and at a good profit, help collect every penny of insurance money owed, but most importantly, she helped both of them deal with the loss of his mother. For that, Phillip was extremely grateful. So what if she knew the truth. If there was one person Phillip knew who would believe it and keep it to themselves, it was she.

Just like Phillip and Franky, Sam never uttered a word of what he knew. He keeps to himself his ordeal with Scotty Cooper. Phillip had spent a lot of time with Sam later, and they became very good friends. Still, he was sure that he had not confided everything even to him. Two years ago he also up and moved to somewhere in Wisconsin. He found a nice girl who he married, and they now have a child of their own. He too writes or calls every now and then.

"You ready?" asked Franky, coming down the hall.

"Ready," said Philip. He reached over and grabbed his coat off the back of the chair. He lifted up the two tickets that lay there and headed out the door leaving nothing on the table except the copy of a cheap magazine. It was opened to the last page where the article below appeared.

Two Murdered In Old Irish Haunted House.

Dublin police are baffled by the strange murder of two local youths found in the closet of a house that once belonged to known Satanist Lord Banthom. Legend has it that Banthom was lynched in the seventeen hundreds by people of the town. One victim, an unidentified male, was hung upside down with his throat slashed, the other victim, an unidentified female, appeared to be half eaten by some large animal . . .

The End

ABOUT THE AUTHOR

Rodney Wetzel was raised in Michigan, graduated with high honors from Western Michigan University, attended Spring Arbor College, and worked in the field of vocational rehabilitation. After a near-fatal car accident in 1995, Rodney began writing as a form of rehabilitation. He and his wife reside outside Tampa, Florida, where he is hard at work on the sequel to Fritz.

Printed in the United States
By Bookmasters